QUINNY & HOPPER

PARTNERS IN
SLIME

QUINNY & HOPPER

Partners in Slime

Written by Adriana Brad Schanen
Illustrated by Charles Santoso

DISNEY • HYPERION
Los Angeles • New York

First Hardcover Edition, October 2016
First Paperback Edition, September 2017
FAC-025438-17202
Printed in the United States of America

Arial MT Pro, Century Schoolbook Pro, Courier New, Vladimir
Script LT Std/Monotype; Billy Serif, Bradley Hand, Feltpen Pro,
Myriad Tilt/Fontspring; Typography of Coop/House Industries

Designed by Tyler Nevins

Library of Congress Control Number for Hardcover: 2016015025
ISBN 978-1-4847-7822-7

Visit www.DisneyBooks.com

For Raymond Peter and Zoe Elizabeth

Much gratitude and love to Julia,
Madeline, Glen and Bubu.
And special thanks to my partners in
slimy research—Liliana Kovacevic, Sarah Geiger,
Jason Kirschner and Jen Savitch.

QUINNY & HOPPER

PARTNERS IN
SLIME

One

Hopper

Today I have to miss school and go see a man who scares me. His name is Dr. Merkle.

"Hopper, are you awake?"

It's Mom at my bedroom door. "I'm up," I mumble.

But I take a long time getting dressed.

I take a really long time chewing my breakfast, which has no taste.

Mom looks at me with a soft face. "Oh, Hopper. It's going to be okay."

Dad looks at me with a harder face. "Ready to go, buddy?"

No, but I don't have much of a choice.

On the way to Dr. Merkle's office, our minivan passes the bus headed to Whisper Valley Elementary School. That bus is full of kids who get to have a normal day. I see my next-door neighbor Quinny riding in her usual seat. My usual seat is right next to hers, but today it's empty. Quinny's bouncing around and talking to all the kids behind her and in front of her and across the aisle. She's talented at talking in every direction. I wave up at her, but she's too busy to notice me.

Then the school bus turns right, and our minivan turns left.

The sign on Dr. Merkle's door says: ISAIAH MERKLE, MD—ENT ASSOCIATES OF GREATER WHISPER VALLEY. *MD* stands for "Medical Doctor" and *ENT* stands for "Ear, Nose, Throat." When you become a doctor, you get to pick which body parts you want to study a little extra and become an expert on. (I like feet, brains, and teeth the most, but Grandpa Gooley says I have a few more years to decide.)

Dad pushes open the door and we walk in.

"Hi there, Hopper," says Trudy at the desk, who has kind brown eyes with bright blue eyelids.

We know each other because I've been here before, lots of times.

We wait in the waiting room. Then we wait some more in the exam room. I shiver a little. It's always chilly in here. Then Dr. Merkle finally comes in. If you replaced the *Dr.* with a *Mr.*, he wouldn't even be that scary. But in his cold office, in his bright white coat, he's slightly terrifying.

"Good morning, Hopper." He smiles straight at me, with teeth as white as his coat. "How's it going today?"

Not so great, or I wouldn't be here.

"Open up and let's have a look."

I open up, and Dr. Merkle looks down my throat. Keeping

my mouth open this wide feels like I'm choking, but I'm used to it.

"Well, Hopper, you've got the biggest tonsils I've ever seen in an eight-year-old kid."

Actually, I'm about to turn nine soon, but I don't bother correcting him.

What Dr. Merkle said sounds impressive, but it just means I breathe funny when I sleep and I get sore throats sometimes (like last week).

"Folks, I really think it's time." Dr. Merkle looks from me to my parents.

He says if I want my sleep to improve and my throat to finally get better, I'll have to go to the hospital and have an operation called a tonsillectomy.

I hear the words *hospital* and *operation*. My ears suddenly feel clogged. Dr. Merkle's voice sounds like someone threw a blanket over his head. The whole world sounds muffled.

"Okay," says Dad. "Let's do it. Let's get this taken care of, once and for all."

"Okay," says Mom, sounding less sure.

"No thank you," I say.

But Dr. Merkle keeps talking. He says a

tonsillectomy is when a doctor removes your tonsils. Everybody is born with two tonsils in the back of their throat. Tonsils are supposed to help keep you healthy by catching germs. But sometimes the tonsils themselves get sick and swell up. Dr. Merkle goes on and on, even though I know this stuff already. I read about tonsillectomies with Mom last year. I wish he would stop talking. I just want to go home.

"Hopper, listen. A tonsillectomy is a simple procedure. Thousands of kids get one every year."

Simple? Maybe a tonsillectomy is simple for the person doing the tonsillectomy.

But the person having his very own tonsils chopped out of his throat might disagree.

"Did you ever have one?" I asked Dr. Merkle.

He smiles again, which is not an answer.

My parents are talking now, too, in between Dr. Merkle's talking.

Mom's words say: "It'll be okay, sweetie. We'll get through this."

But her face says: *There's a chance it won't be okay, and I'm as scared as you are.*

Dad's words say: "No worries, Hopper. You've got this."

But his face says: *Calm down; don't panic; don't be such a wimp.*

What people say with their faces is as important as what they say with their words.

Then Dr. Merkle asks if I have any other questions about the tonsillectomy.

"When you say 'remove' . . . you mean with a knife?" I picture a knife in my throat.

"It's not a knife, Hopper. I'll be using a small, precise surgical tool called a Coblator."

"Will it hurt?"

"You'll be asleep the whole time. Then your throat will be sore for a few days. It'll hurt to swallow at first, but you'll get to have lots of Popsicles and ice cream as you heal."

That last part sounds okay. I try to trust Dr. Merkle. The diploma on his wall says he's been an ENT doctor for eighteen years. That's twice as long as I've been alive. That's a lot of tonsils.

"So how does Friday morning sound?" he says.

"This Friday?" I try to keep my voice normal. "You mean the day after tomorrow?"

"No reason to wait, Hopper," he says. "The less time for you to worry, the better."

Mom and Dad both chuckle at this, but I don't see what's so funny.

When we get home, I ask Mom, "Can I go on the computer?"

She looks at me carefully. "Hopper, if you have more tonsillectomy questions, we can call Dr. Merkle or figure out the answers together. Sound good?"

I don't want to make Mom feel worse by letting her know how scared I really am. "That's okay. I'm fine. I'm going upstairs for a while."

I go up and sit on my bed and open *Atlas of Human Anatomy* by Frank H. Netter.

It's the heaviest book I own, and my favorite, full of drawings of the insides of human bodies— technical, detailed pictures that real doctors use. I turn to a page with tonsils on it. I look at the drawings. There's so much going on inside our bodies that we can't see. I used to think it was incredible. But now I wish my insides were made of steel.

I pull out my chess set. Chess is a great way to

turn off your feelings. I usually play both sides of the game, since no one else in my family is interested in chess, and since both of me are free at the same time. I wait for this game of chess to fill up my whole mind and push out all my feelings. But it doesn't.

I wish Dad didn't think I was such a wimp.

I wish I could tell Mom how scared I really am.

I wish it were already Saturday and the tonsil operation were over.

Then some banging on my door interrupts all my wishing.

"Hopper, Hopper, Hopper!" cries Quinny's voice. "Can I come in?"

Before I answer, she bursts in and plops on my bed. "Hopper, guess what! Today I colored a math sheet that turned into a puppy, and for cursive I got to write 'cookie' twenty-five times, and then I saw a blue jay on the playground, which is Piper's favorite bird."

"Hi, Quinny."

"Plus I have your homework from Ms. Yoon. Plus tomorrow is the thrilling, amazing trip to the animal shelter. I'm so glad you'll be back for that. Plus also, congratulations!"

"What for?"

"I just heard you have the biggest tonsils ever!"

"So what? It's not like I get a prize or anything."

"You never know."

"What's the homework?"

Instead of telling me, she looks at my chess set. "Hey, can I play, too?"

"Sure, why not."

I've tried to teach Quinny how to play chess a bunch of times. But I guess there are two kinds of people in the world: chess people and checkers people. Sometimes I let her win, just to see more of her smile, but usually she wanders away before we get too far.

"Hey, are you hungry?" She pops up from the game. "I'm starving. Let's get a snack."

I follow her downstairs. Mom fixes us cheese and crackers and apple slices. I pour us water.

"Open wide," Quinny says as we start to eat. "I want to see your tonsils."

"No thank you."

"Please? Pretty please? Pretty please with tonsil slime on top?"

"That's disgusting."

"Come on, let me see."

There's no use arguing when Quinny gets this excited. I open wide.

"Hopper, look! There they are!" she cries.

"Aaaahh caaan't luuuk," I remind her, because I don't have eyeballs inside my throat.

"Oh, they're so cute—they look like little turkey meatballs."

Suddenly I'm not hungry anymore. My food sits there as Quinny gobbles hers down.

"Hey, if you're not going to eat that, can I have it?" she asks.

I push my plate in her direction. Quinny eats all my crackers and says, "You know, Hopper, you're so lucky you get to go to the hospital. I haven't been there in ages."

"Are you kidding? The hospital is where people get sick and die."

"It's also where people get better and babies get born," she says. "Plus afterward, your mom

10

said you'll get to eat all the pistachio ice cream and Popsicles you want—in bed!"

I'll believe it when I see the pistachio ice cream.

"Quinny, I hear you're excited about the class trip to the animal shelter," says Mom, changing the subject away from tonsils.

"Oh yes, Mrs. Grey, it's going to be incredible. My teacher, Ms. Yoon, said there will be dozens of wonderful, beautiful, homeless cats and dogs, and I want to sign up to volunteer and take care of them, and then my parents will realize how mature and responsible I am and finally let me get a dog even though Piper is allergic—"

"That's great, Quinny," says Mom. "Good luck with all that."

Then my big brothers, Ty and Trevor, walk in. They're dirty and sweaty from soccer practice. Mom makes them leave their giant, muddy cleats by the back door. But there's nothing she can do about their giant, stinky feet.

Ty grabs my shoulder hello. Trevor yanks my ear hello.

Quinny moves away when they try to bother

her hair hello. She makes a growly face, but they laugh. My brothers' thick, sporty bodies fill the kitchen, and they both start telling Mom how a teammate wrenched his knee at soccer practice.

If Quinny and I sneak out right now, maybe they'll leave us alone. I gesture to her. She nods. We slip out of the kitchen.

"Ooh, I have a great idea," says Quinny. "Let's go play with Disco and Cha-Cha."

"I'm kind of tired."

"Okay, well, don't worry. I fed them this morning and explained why you weren't around today, and they totally understood."

I doubt they understood. Because Disco and Cha-Cha are chickens.

We help take care of them at our neighbor Mrs. Porridge's house. They're just a few weeks old and not fully feathered yet, so they're living inside her screened-in porch. Mrs. Porridge actually pays us to take care of them. But she pays us in eggs. And since Disco and Cha-Cha won't lay any eggs until they're older, we haven't gotten our first paycheck yet.

"Hey, Quinny," I say. "Don't tell people."

"What?"

"I don't want the kids in school to know about my tonsils and the operation."

"What's the big deal?"

"Just promise me you won't tell everybody in school, okay?"

"Okay, fine."

But the next morning, by the lockers, guess what people are talking about.

Alex Delgado says, "I went to the hospital when I fell out of a tree. They have electric beds that go up and down and fold in half. Be careful you don't get crushed inside one."

Caleb says, "We went to visit my aunt at the hospital and got lost. The place is huge!"

Victoria says, "Aren't you kind of old to be having your tonsils out? I had mine out when I was five. I heard the older you are, the more painful it is." She says this with a smile. The tips of her hair are pink. Her nails are striped black and white. Victoria is the kind of person who never usually talks to me, which I don't mind one bit.

After morning meeting, Ms. Yoon announces

that we need to get ready and line up for the trip to the animal shelter. Lots of kids make excited noises. Quinny's are the loudest.

I get in line behind her. "Thanks a lot," I whisper into her ear.

"You're welcome," Quinny says, and then she turns around. "Wait, Hopper, what for?"

"You told everybody in school about my operation!" I whisper-shout.

"I did not."

"Did too!"

"Did not, I just told *one* person, not everybody. And it wasn't even in school. I was *outside* of school while we were walking from the bus, and it was only Caleb, who's your friend, too, so I don't see what the big deal is—"

"The big deal is Caleb told Alex Delgado, who told Victoria, who told everyone."

"Then you should be mad at them, not me," says Quinny. "And why do you always say Alex-Delgado, like it's all one word? He's the only Alex in third grade."

"Stop changing the subject," I tell her.

"Stop trying to keep everything a secret."

"I don't."

"You do! You tried to keep me a secret from your brothers all summer. You keep your personality a secret in school. I'm sorry, but you can't keep your giant tonsils a secret—they're just too exciting!"

Quinny's words shoot deep into my ears and swirl around my head. They make my eyes blur. They make my face burn. Quinny doesn't like it that I'm quiet. Well, I don't like it that she's loud. We shouldn't even be friends in the first place, but it happened when she moved in next door to me over the summer. It happened before I knew any better. And walking away from a friend like her is harder than it looks.

"I don't see what the big deal is." Quinny keeps talking. "Everyone's going to find out when you're absent anyway. Lots of kids have their tonsils out."

"The big deal is you promised not to tell. You're a liar."

Quinny's eyebrows twist. She leans over and whisper-shouts into my ear: "And you're a wimpy scaredy-pants who whines about everything!"

"Quinny? Hopper? Is everything okay?"

Ms. Yoon is standing above us now. Her big, round belly has a baby inside it. Way above her giant belly is her tiny head, which looks concerned. "Quinny, please come with me," she says. "Everyone else, please follow Mr. Sellars to the bus."

Quinny looks confused, but Ms. Yoon's tone of voice is firm. I watch them walk away.

Then Quinny turns around and sticks her tongue out at me.

Mr. Sellars, another third-grade teacher, leads the rest of us toward the bus for the field trip. I follow my class outside. I get on the bus with everybody.

Everybody except Quinny.

I look back at the school building. Where is she?

The bus driver starts the engine. Mr. Sellars reminds everybody to buckle up.

Maybe Quinny is in trouble. Good, she deserves it. But I wonder if I'm the one who got her into trouble. What if I just made her miss the best field trip of her life?

The bus driver revs the engine. The whole bus rumbles and vibrates.

"Mr. Sellars?" I call out. "Mr. Sellars?"

But he's looking at a clipboard and talking to some kids at the front of the bus. I unbuckle my seat belt and rush up to him. "Mr. Sellars, Quinny Bumble is not on the bus."

"I'm aware of that, Hopper," he says without looking up from his clipboard. "Now please go back to your seat."

Two

Quinny

I don't know why Ms. Yoon is dragging me away from the bus for that amazing field trip to the animal shelter, which is a trip I've been looking forward to every minute of every day since she told us about it a few weeks ago.

"Ms. Yoon, I'm supposed to be getting on the bus for that amazing field trip!"

"Hold your horses, Quinny. There's something we have to do first."

"Can't we do it later? For example, after the field trip? Because this might be my only chance to play with a puppy, or it can even be a grown-up dog. I'm not picky, because I've wanted a dog for so long, but my parents keep bringing home little sisters instead—"

"Yes, Quinny, you've mentioned this once or twice before."

"Plus I want to sign up to volunteer with the animals, too, because all those poor homeless animals have nobody and nothing, and I just *know* I could cheer them up."

But Ms. Yoon leads us around the corner and down the hall, and I suddenly realize this is the way to Principal Ramsey's office.

"Wait, Ms. Yoon, I'm sorry. I didn't mean to yell at Hopper—"

"I know—"

"I'm very, very, extra-very sorry. Please don't report me to the principal!"

"Quinny, take a breath."

"Or, if you're mad about the thing with Victoria at recess, it wasn't my fault. That yard guard–playground lady did not see the whole thing! I really, truly, absolutely did *not* trip Victoria on purpose. My foot was there first—"

"I hear you—"

"Or, if you're upset about my *how-to* project, I promise I'll definitely find a new topic that is one hundred percent appropriate."

"I know you will, Quinny."

Earlier this week we all had to figure out topics for our *how-to-do-or-make-something* writing projects for language arts, and mine was *How to Get My Sister Piper to Stop Peeing Her Pants at Night.*

Piper just turned five last month and has a very small bladder (plus a very sneaky personality, but that's a different problem). I had this idea for hooking her mattress up to an alarm that would ring when she pees on it—like the opposite of a fire alarm—and I thought this would be a great topic. But Ms. Yoon pulled me aside and said Piper's bed-wetting is her own personal business, which isn't true, since it makes my parents super tired and cranky to me in the mornings. I guess Ms. Yoon talked to my parents, too, because that night they did this whole ultralong lecture about *privacy* and *respect* and how big sisters should treat little sisters. But I already know how to treat Piper. I read to her all the time (someone's got to help that kid learn proper English). I play cards and games with her, even though she cheats. I let her jump in the tub with me, even though her grimy feet turn the water brown. Just once I'd like my parents to do a lecture about how little sisters should treat big sisters (rule number one: No using your spit as a weapon) because *she's* the one who starts all the trouble.

Anyway, I'm about to tell Ms. Yoon that I've come up with an even more brilliant *how-to* idea—"How to Raise Chickens in Your Backyard"—but she holds up her hand.

"Quinny, I can assure you, this isn't about your *how-to* assignment, nor your difficulties with Victoria. Nurse Mira actually needs to see you."

"Nurse Mira? Why me? I'm not even sick."

"We're almost there. She'll explain."

"I promise I'm not sick! Look, I'll prove it. I'll do a cartwheel. See, I'm fine!"

I turn a happy cartwheel right there in the hall, to prove to Ms. Yoon I did not catch that barfy stomach bug that's been going around school.

"Quinny!" she shrieks as my upside-down legs whiz by her, very close.

"Sorry, Ms. Yoon," I apologize through my flustered hair.

"Please check your engine." Her voice is tight now. "And no cartwheels in the hall."

I know that rule. But sometimes I forget the things I already know.

"I'm very, very, extra-very sorry. It won't happen again."

Ms. Yoon leads me to the nurse's office and opens the door, and Nurse Mira is sitting in there with a surprise guest: my little sister Piper.

Piper's hair is messier than usual, and loose from its pigtails. Her cheeks are blotchy. Her eyes look scared.

"What's going on? Piper, are you okay?" I rush over and feel her forehead, like Mom does when we're sick. It does not feel hot. I put my arm around her.

At home, Piper is a pain in the bottom who ruins my life. But at school, she is kind of fun to have around. Almost like a little pet.

"Quinny, I'm afraid I need to do a head check," says Nurse Mira.

She comes at me with a magnifying glass.

Phooey. Not again. Some kids in my grade had fleas last month, so we all had to get our heads checked. But I was fine.

"Nurse Mira, you mean Piper has fleas?" I pull away from that little sister.

"They're called lice, Quinny, and yes, we found a live bug and several nits, or lice eggs, on Piper's head," she says. "And now we need to check your head, too."

"But I don't have lice! I'm not itchy or scratchy or anything!"

"It's school policy. Just to make sure."

I let her pick through my hair. I hear the bus engine growl to a start outside.

"Please hurry! The bus is going to the animal shelter exactly right now!"

But Nurse Mira does not hurry. When she's finally done poking and pulling, my hair has swelled up to twice its normal size. She goes to talk to Ms. Yoon by the door, and they take *forever.* Then she comes around to me. "I'm afraid I have bad news, Quinny."

Even before she tells me, I know: I won't be getting on that bus.

I start crying, and Piper comes over and hugs me, and she's crying, too. I'm so shocked to lose my big, beautiful field trip that I forget to blame her for giving me fleas.

I just slump there, holding on to my pesky little sister who ruined my life. It's not as good as hugging a dog, but it'll have to do.

Three

Hopper

It's the night before my tonsillectomy, and Dad brings home a cake.

The frosting on top of the cake says *Good-bye, Tonsils.*

"So long," says Dad. "It's been *swell* knowing you."

I'm not sure if he is talking about my swollen tonsils or all of me. But then he elbows me and I realize I'm supposed to chuckle at his joke.

"Relax, Hopper, everything's going to be okay," says Mom, picking up a knife and aiming it at the cake. "It'll be over before you know it."

It will. The operation. And maybe my life, too.

Trevor and Ty are excited about the cake. They surround it. They lean over and breathe on it.

I am not excited. I don't see the point of eating cake to celebrate something awful, so I go upstairs to my room.

Mom and Dad follow me. They try to talk to me about my feelings. (Again.)

It is a short conversation because I only have one feeling right now, and it's this: I do not want to have a tonsillectomy. Not tomorrow, not ever.

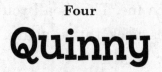

Four

Quinny

Daddy picks us up from school and promises we'll go to the animal shelter another time, but he won't say exactly when. I know a wishy-washy promise when I hear one.

"When? When exactly can we go? How about now? I'm free right now!"

"Quinny, cut it out. We have to deal with the lice first."

"You're never going to take me there, are you?"

"Not if you keep acting like this."

"See, I knew it!"

On the ride home, Piper tries to snuggle with me in the backseat, but I push her away.

"Don't touch me. This is all your fault!"

She wiggles back to me again, so I poke her just a bit, very gently.

"Quinny hitted me!" she bellows.

"I did not! She won't get off me!"

"Quinny, please!" yells Daddy from up front.

All my friends got to visit cats and dogs today, while all I got were fleas from my little twit-ster. The UNFAIRNESS of it all stings my whole body with icy-hot pain. I feel like pinching Piper. But I don't, because I'm the oldest, so I have to SET A GOOD EXAMPLE. (Which is even *more* unfair.)

But then, as Daddy pulls into our driveway, I remember something interesting. Last month McKayla, my friend at school, got lice, too. And she went to see this lady called the Lice Lady. McKayla said that, at the Lice Lady's house, you get to sit in a big, cushy chair and watch cartoons and drink punch while she combs conditioner that smells like flowers through your hair. And then you get this cool braided hairstyle that stays in your hair for a whole week. And this all sounded so great that nobody even felt bad for McKayla for getting lice—not even Victoria. So I tell Daddy about the Lice Lady. And he looks her up.

But it turns out that a trip to the Lice Lady is expensive.

Very, very, extra-very expensive.

So Daddy decides he's just going to read the pamphlet from Nurse Mira and handle the whole situation himself at home.

First he pours mouthwash all over my head in the bathroom sink. My hair has never had such fresh breath in its whole life!

Then he closes the lid to the toilet and sits me down and squeezes goopy-slimy white conditioner all over my head and picks and combs through my hair for approximately seventeen thousand hours in a row while barking at me to hold still.

Holding still is not one of my strengths.

"Quinny, stop wiggling." Daddy pulls at my hair with a pinchy, tight comb.

"I'm not wiggling. The toilet seat is wiggling."

Piper plays in the bathtub, waiting her turn. Cleo, our baby sister, is in the next room, sitting in front of a Muppets video. I can hear her giggling. I don't much feel like giggling.

Piper splashes my foot and says, "Last night ago, you promised to read me a pitcher book and you forgotted."

I make a ferocious face toward the bathtub. "There's no such thing as a *pitcher* book. And *forgotted* isn't a word. I can't believe they let you into kindergarten."

"Quinny, hold still!" Daddy tugs at my hair. "And be nice."

"How come she gets a bath while I have to sit on the toilet?"

Piper splashes around again, in a braggy way, and I notice she's not just splashing. She's putting foam numbers up on the wall around the tub, making complicated addition and subtraction sums. Three, four, and five numbers at a time.

$4 + 6 + 1 - 2 - 3 = 6$.

Piper = show-off.

This is not normal math for a measly five-year-old. Piper wasn't even supposed to go to my school this year. She turned five on September 4, which means she's too young to be in kindergarten. But she was driving her pre-K teacher nuts with pesky questions, and then at home she kept trying to do *my* math sheets, and so my parents decided she was ready to start kindergarten after all. So now Piper rides the bus with me and Hopper to Whisper Valley Elementary School every day. But at home, she still runs around our yard like a half-naked, barefoot baboon and pees outside by her special tree, and she still can't speak proper

English. I think my sister is part monkey, part evil genius.

"I got one!" says Daddy, holding up a speck from my hair and looking proud.

I can't look. That poor dead flea is just a tiny, sad smear on the paper towel now.

Then Mom gets home from work and takes over my head so Daddy can go put all our bed stuff in the dryer and vacuum the whole house (which the lice booklet from Nurse Mira said to do).

Mom picks through my hair, sighing and snapping at me to hold still, too.

That's when I notice Piper out in the hall, squirting a big bottle of gloopy white conditioner onto the soles of her feet. Which definitely don't have fleas.

"Quinny, hold still."

"Uh, Mom? Look, I think Piper's turning herself into a human Slip'n Slide."

Piper zooms down the long hallway on her slippery feet. Naked and laughing.

Mom bolts from the bathroom.

Next there's yelling. Lots of yelling and crying.

And the sound of a mop sloshing and squeaking. I sit tight on the toilet seat, the only well-behaved child this family's got.

Mom comes back and keeps picking through my hair. Her face is sweaty and droopy. When she's all done, she hands me a shower cap. A big, puffy, crinkly shower cap that I'm supposed to put over my slimy hair so I don't smear the world.

I stretch that noisy cap over my head and stare at myself in the bathroom mirror.

I look like a mini lunch lady now.

And then, because this is an extremely unlucky day for me, the doorbell rings, just as I'm washing goopy conditioner off my hands, and Mom calls out, "Quinny, it's for you!"

Which is a shock, because who on earth could be visiting me right now?

With my unlucky luck, it's probably Victoria, who sometimes visits her great-aunt, Mrs. Porridge, who lives down the street from us. I picture Victoria's face looking at my slimy hair in this shower cap. I picture her little mouth twisting into a smile, and her words rubbing it in that I missed the field trip and all the amazing animals.

I hear noise coming from downstairs and lock the bathroom door.

I can't let Victoria see me like this. She's nice to me half the time and not nice the other half— and I never know which half I'm going to get.

"Quinny, Hopper's brothers are here," Mom calls up. "They'd like to talk to you."

What in the world do Trevor and Ty want with me?

Mom sends those big twin bullies thumping upstairs. I peek out at them from the bathroom. "What do you want?"

"We need your help," says Trevor (or is it Ty?).

"We need your help, big-time," adds Ty (or Trevor—I can't tell).

I figure this is either a joke or a trap. I come out of the bathroom to find out which.

"Dad got Hopper a cake 'cause his tonsils are getting sliced off tomorrow. But he won't come down to eat it, and Mom won't let us have any till he goes first," says Trevor/Ty.

"Your mission, should you choose to accept it, is to get him out of his room and get him downstairs and get some cake in his face," says Ty/Trevor.

"I can't. I have lice."

"No duh. But you're wearing a shower cap," says one of those bullyheads.

"I'm not supposed to go near people until I get my head checked again."

"Trust me, it's okay—we had lice last year," says the other bullyhead.

"And the year before," says the other-other one. "We know what we're talking about. Just keep the cap on and it won't be a problem."

I don't trust these bully twins. But I can't think of a good reason not to help Hopper. He really could use more cake in his life. I look out my bedroom window, but his window shade is pulled all the way down. Not a good sign. I hate the idea of him sitting there feeling sad or scared. Everything's going to be okay tomorrow. I wish he knew that. (Also, I should probably say sorry for calling him a wimpy scaredy-pants at school. I didn't mean it. I was just mad he called me a liar.)

"Okay," I say. "I accept the mission."

"Great!" says Ty/Trevor.

"Now, listen up, there's more," says Trevor/Ty.

They come closer. We get in a huddle, kind of like football players on TV.

"The doctor said he can't eat for twelve hours before his operation. So you've got exactly thirty-four minutes to get over there, get him out of his room, and shove some cake in his face."

"What flavor is the cake?" I ask.

"Huh? That's not important."

"Of course it's important. And how many pieces do I get to take home?"

"None!" both bullyheads bellow at once.

"It's been nice chatting with you." I back away.

"Okay, okay, it's chocolate-chocolate and you can have one piece."

"Three giant pieces," I say. "One for me, and one for each of my sisters."

This is called negotiating.

"But one of your sisters is just a baby," points out T/T.

"The price is now up to five pieces of cake. One for everyone in my family."

"Two small pieces, and we'll throw in some soccer lessons."

"Whoopee." I twirl my finger.

"Don't try to play it cool," says T/T. "We know you watch us practice in our yard. You want to play soccer. It's obvious."

I would never admit this to Hopper, but the bully twins are kind of right. After all, kicking is one of my strengths. And I'll be out of belts to try for in tae kwon do pretty soon.

"We could teach you. We're awesome."

"Three pieces or no deal," I say. "Now, shoo, go away and let me think."

I go back into my room and think hard about how to make Hopper cheer up and eat some tonsil cake. I pretend my shower cap is really a thinking cap.

I start a list of things he likes doing—or, at least, likes watching me do:

1) Cantaloupe bowling. (The trick is to use plastic bottles of salad dressing, not glass ones, for bowling pins.)
2) Dance party with Disco and Cha-Cha. (One of these days I'll get Hopper to dance, too, instead of just watching me and the chickens dance.)
3) Feed my baby sister, Cleo, a pickle. (She makes the best faces.)

Then I think of something even better to cheer Hopper up. I drag a chair to my closet and climb onto my tippy-toes and reach across the top shelf for a square brown envelope.

Inside is a secret surprise I've been saving for his birthday.

But this is an emergency. The twins need my help right now. Hopper needs my help. I am on a mission.

Five

Hopper

Three knocks, then a brown envelope slides under my door, covered in scribbles.

Dear Hopper, Sorry I told Caleb about your tonsils. I had a crummy day, and I know you did, too. The solution is CAKE!! Plus here's a surprise that will cheer you up for sure. Also, please tell me all about that animal field trip, too!!!

Your friend, Quinny

"Hopper, I know you're in there," calls Quinny from the hallway. "Hurry up and open that envelope, and also, please forgive me? Plus did you know that tonsil cake downstairs is chocolate-chocolate. Doesn't it sound delicious?"

I lean against my door, just in case Quinny decides to barge in here without my permission. I don't want to open this envelope in front of her. I don't like audiences.

"Hopper?" She pushes on the door. "Oh, Hopper . . ."

I push back. She pushes harder and grunts. Finally, I step away, and the door whips open and Quinny tumbles in with a gasp.

"Sneaky!" She laughs.

"Quinny, why are you wearing a shower cap?"

"So nobody catches my fleas. My head laid some flea eggs, so Nurse Mira sent me home early."

I shrink back from her.

"Don't worry. I'm pretty sure Daddy killed them all with mouthwash. Open the envelope! I was saving it for your birthday, but I heard you need some emergency cheering up. And then tell me all about the animals on that field trip, please!"

Before I can say anything, Quinny keeps talking.

"Tell me: How many dogs did you see? What

kinds? Were they all in cages? Did any of them look perfect for me? Wait—OPEN THE ENVELOPE FIRST!"

"Okay, okay." I tear it open.

Inside is a paper in the shape of a brain. Two paper brains, actually, and each says:

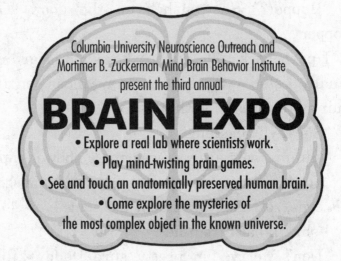

Columbia University Neuroscience Outreach and
Mortimer B. Zuckerman Mind Brain Behavior Institute
present the third annual

BRAIN EXPO

- Explore a real lab where scientists work.
- Play mind-twisting brain games.
- See and touch an anatomically preserved human brain.
- Come explore the mysteries of
the most complex object in the known universe.

I stand there and read the paper brain again. I can't breathe I'm so excited.

"Happy birthday in advance!" says Quinny. "The best part is, I'm going with you! It's on a Sunday afternoon in New York City in just a few weeks, and we're going to touch a real brain, which is the weirdest thing ever!"

I can't think of any words to say to this. "Thank you, Quinny," I finally whisper.

"But wait! There's more! We're also going to Central Park, which used to be my backyard, and the Hungarian Pastry Shop, my favorite place for treats in New York. They have cream puffs and poppy seed Danish and soft, flaky cherry strudel that's way better than Toaster Strudel, and hey—you see what I'm doing here? I bet you haven't thought about your tonsils once since I got here. I bet all this talking is making you hungry. You're starving for some cake, aren't you? Let's go grab some before those bully twins eat it all!"

"No thank you. Could you please stop trying to cheer me up now?"

"Okay, I'll stop." Quinny takes my hand. "C'mon."

Just because a person goes downstairs doesn't mean he really wants to.

Just because a person eats tonsil cake doesn't mean he's actually enjoying it.

Just because a person forgets he's upset for a moment doesn't mean he's cheered up.

But that cake is pretty good, I have to admit.

My brothers wolf it down, with crumbs dribbling from their mouths. Quinny groans as she eats hers, like she's dying of happiness.

"Nice work." Trevor boxes Quinny's arm.

"We didn't think you could pull it off," says Ty, licking his plate.

"It was a piece of cake!" Quinny laughs, but then stops when I frown at her.

Afterward, Mom wraps up some cake for Quinny to take home.

"Two pieces only," Ty tells Mom.

"Three, please. A deal's a deal," Quinny says. "Mrs. Grey, can Hopper walk me home?"

Quinny doesn't need someone to walk her right next door, but she grabs my arm and pulls me along before I can point this out. "Let's take the long way!" she suggests.

We zig through my yard, zag through hers, then walk toward her back door. I slow down because I don't want this night to be over. Just because a person is quiet doesn't mean he always likes keeping his feelings inside.

"You're lucky you don't have to go to the hospital tomorrow," I say to Quinny.

"You're lucky you're getting all this attention," she says. "That cake was yummy!"

But I don't have any room in my head to feel lucky. It's clogged with *what-if*s.

"What if my tonsils are so big the doctor can't get them out of my throat?" I ask.

"Easy. He'll just slice and dice them up like stir-fry!"

"What if they're so slippery he drops them down my throat by mistake? What if I wake up in the middle of the operation? What if I don't even get to the operation because the hospital bed crushes me, like Alex Delgado said?"

"You mean Alex."

"What if the hospital is so big that my parents get lost and can't find me? What if—"

"What if we go have a dance party RIGHT NOW?" Quinny pulls me into a run.

"Quinny, no." But her hand won't let mine go.

"C'mon, you didn't see them at all this morning—they miss you! Hey, do you think chickens like cake? There's only one way to find out!"

* * *

45

The minute we walk onto Mrs. Porridge's screened-in porch, Disco and Cha-Cha start *brrrrr*-ing and *bipp*-ing. Quinny turns on the porch light, and they jump off their mini-roost.

Walter the cat comes over, too, and growls. He sleeps out here to protect Cha-Cha. He's never glad to see us.

Quinny shows off the tonsil cake. "Who wants a piece of me?"

The chickens flap and flutter. Walter stays by Cha-Cha. When Disco gets close to them, Walter hisses. "Hey, kiddos, play nice!" says Quinny. "No cake for meanies."

Mrs. Porridge comes out onto the porch in her robe. "What is this racket? Didn't anyone ever tell you children it's polite to knock before riling up a neighbor's chickens?"

"Hi, Mrs. Porridge. Hopper's worried about his tonsils, so we're cheering him up."

"Hopper, I knew Dr. Merkle's mother. She raised a fine son," Mrs. Porridge tells me. "You're in good hands. Everything will be fine tomorrow."

"You don't know that," I say. "Bad things happen all the time. I watch the news."

"You're too young to be watching the news," Mrs. Porridge says. "And, Quinny, put that cake away. It's not good for chickens."

"What about dancing? That's good for chickens. Mrs. Porridge, turn on some music!"

"Oh, please, it's too late for that nonsense."

"Just one song and we'll get out of your hair. 'Twist and Shout' by the Beatles?"

Mrs. Porridge snorts. Quinny begs.

I finally find the guts to say my biggest *what-if* out loud. I touch Quinny's arm to get her attention. "What if I don't wake up from the operation?"

Quinny doesn't answer right away. I wait for her to make a joke.

"Then I won't have anyone to go to the Brain Expo with," she says quietly. "So you just *have* to wake up, or those tickets will go to waste. Okay?"

I look at Mrs. Porridge, who shrugs. "The girl makes a lot of sense."

"Okay." I shrug, too.

Then Mrs. Porridge puts on "Twist and Shout," and Quinny twists and shouts and wiggles with those chickens. Last year, Victoria Porridge did

ballet for our school talent show.
(I wasn't in the show, but Mom
took me to go watch.)
Quinny's danc-
ing is the exact
opposite of that.
The whole time,
it looks like she's
about to lose her
balance and fall
down, but she
never does.
I watch her
dance, and it
really is okay. Between the cake and the chickens
and Quinny and Mrs. Porridge, I actually feel better than okay.

But when I open my eyes the next morning, I feel
scared all over again.

It's still dark when we leave the house. Dad
tries to carry me to the car in my pj's, but I tell
him I'll walk. I'm no baby. (I wish I were, though;
then it would be okay to cry.)

I hold on to my blanket during the ride, even though I know it can't protect me.

The hospital parking lot is empty. Like we're the only people left on Earth.

Inside, I sit in a hard chair in a row of empty hard chairs. My parents fill out forms at a counter. A bracelet snaps onto my wrist and won't come off no matter how hard I tug.

My parents walk me to a small room, and there is a skinny bed where I have to get undressed and put on a hospital gown with bunnies on it. I don't even like bunnies. I wish they had a hospital gown with fish on it. Or chickens. Or Quinny's face.

No, not Quinny's face. That would be weird.

We wait in this small room. A man with spiky hair and a name tag that reads NURSE CHUCK comes in, and he's nice, but I don't have the energy to be nice back. He gives me a paper hat to cover my hair. Then a tall lady in a white coat walks in and tells me her name is Dr. Parva, which is also on her name tag. She has a gentle face and a steady voice, and she says it is her job to make me sleep during the operation and wake up afterward. It's not the same kind of sleep you do at night; it's a deeper kind, where you breathe in from this mask to *fall unconscious*. I've never done that before. Dr. Parva says it won't hurt. She says I won't remember any of it, and when I wake up, my parents will be there with me. She offers me the mask, and asks if I want to try it out, just to see what it's like.

"No thank you."

But then I change my mind. I put it near my face, just for a second.

She also tells me that when I wake up, there will be a thin little tube called an IV sticking out of my arm, which is supposed to keep my body from getting thirsty during the surgery. She says that won't hurt, either, and they'll take it out before I go home.

Dr. Merkle comes in next, too friendly as usual. He says he's *delighted* to see me and cracks a joke with Nurse Chuck that I don't understand. He asks if I have any more questions. He says, "Okay, let's get this show on the road."

And then I realize my bed has wheels, because it's moving.

Bars pop up on both sides of it, to keep me from falling out. Or maybe from escaping.

The sun is coming up through a hallway window. Normal people are just waking up now, and I wish I were one of them. Nurse Chuck's eyes crinkle at me as he pushes the bed. I don't know what's going to happen next, but it keeps happening anyway. The bed is moving fast. I grab the bars and we pass through doors that swing and squeak after us. The walls are different now—the light is different. Mom squeezes my hand. Dad nods, even though I didn't say anything for him to agree with. We leave him behind and keep rolling.

The operating room is too bright. It smells too cold. It's crowded with humming, beeping machines that look mean and complicated. There are more people here—masked people in sky-blue ninja-pajama outfits. Everyone has just half a face: eyes and a forehead. Are they all here for me? I don't like this. I don't like audiences. I want to run away.

Dr. Parva is here and she tells me to breathe deeply into the mask. Mom squeezes my hand so tight now that it hurts. This is the hardest thing I've ever had to do, but I'm not going to cry, because then she'll cry. I squeeze Mom's hand back. I don't want her to let go of me, ever. I don't want that mask to come down on my face, ever.

But here it comes.

Six

Quinny

SCREEEE SCREEEEE SCREEEEE.

A weird, screechy cackle wakes me up. It's not Piper, because we don't share a room anymore. (One thing I don't miss about our old apartment in New York: Piper's slobbery snores.) I can't tell what that noise is, so I go and open my window.

SCREEEEEEE. It's coming from the air itself, like it's everywhere.

But then it stops. Huh.

After breakfast, I walk over to do my chicken chores, and I hear the noise again.

"Mrs. Porridge, there it is—the noise that woke me. It's coming from Disco's face!"

Mrs. Porridge is drinking coffee on her porch steps. She looks tired. "No kidding."

"Do you think she's sick?" I ask.

"I don't think so."

I look down at Disco, all scruffy and hyper, hopping around on her giant, scaly starfish feet. "Did you lay your first egg and you're spreading the news?"

"SCREEE CREEEEE ZEEEE." Disco puffs out her chest and lifts her tail.

I check the cardboard henhouse, just in case. Nope, no eggs.

"Are you mad about something?"

"Ooop erp CREEEEEEEEEEE."

Disco is bossy and kind of loud in general, I've noticed. She goes especially bonkers whenever Cha-Cha jumps onto Walter for a kitty-back ride.

"Maybe Disco's just doing a chicken burp," says Piper.

I look down at her and roll my eyes. Piper is here helping me today because Hopper is at the hospital. Normally, he and I feed, water, and clean up after the chickens five mornings a week: Tuesday through Saturday. It's a big responsibility, but it's really, truly, absolutely the best part of my day (despite the poop). Plus, if we didn't do it, Mrs. Porridge promised she'd let them starve. (I think she likes to say things just to shock us sometimes.)

"Do you know what's going on with Disco?" I turn to Cha-Cha.

"Wrrrr-bup." Cha-Cha dips her petite pokey head. Then she jumps onto Walter.

The more I take care of these birds, the more I understand what they're saying. They're pullets now—which means teenager in the chick-tionary—and the way they talk is somewhere between baby-chick chirping and grown-up–hen clucking.

"So if Disco isn't sick or mad or excited about an egg, then what is it?" I ask Cha-Cha.

"It sounds like Disco has decided he's a rooster," answers Mrs. Porridge.

"I don't think so. Roosters say 'cock-a-doodle-do.' This noise was different."

"Quinny, roosters have their own way of saying 'cock-a-doodle-do' that's different from the way American humans pronounce it."

"Well, we'll just have to talk her out of being a rooster and back to being a hen!"

"Don't hold your breath. Won't be long before that birdbrained bag of feathers starts waking up the whole neighborhood with his crowing—he's gotta go."

"Mrs. Porridge, no! This is Disco's home! I'll get her to stop—"

"Him. Roosters are male, Quinny—"

"Him, her, whatever. I'll make Disco stop crowing and promise to never do it again."

"Good luck. We are what we are. No amount of conversation's going to change *that*."

Later that morning, Daddy takes me and Piper by Nurse Mira's office at school.

She checks both of our heads with her giant magnified eye. I cross all my fingers and toes until she finally says, "All clear, no bugs. Good job, Mr. Bumble."

"Yay!" Piper and I jump and hug at the same time, which is really painful for my chin.

"Ow!"

Nurse Mira gives my chin an ice pack. She gives us both bandannas. "You girls may want to wear these for now. Keep your heads covered to lower the risk of re-infestation."

The risk of *what*? "You mean the bugs are still out there, Nurse Mira?"

"Better safe than sorry," she says. "A bandanna a day helps keep head lice away."

I tie the bandanna on, but my hair bursts out on the side. I try again, but my hair *boing*s out the other side. Hmmm, I think my head is just too much for this measly bandanna.

At the lockers, I see Victoria. Even worse, she sees me.

"Well, that's a look," she says. "Why didn't you get the cool braids, like McKayla?"

"Argh," says Caleb. "Quinny, you look like a pirate."

I giggle. *"Arrgh!"*

After Hopper, Caleb is my second-favorite friend at school. He's new this year, just like I am. But he doesn't let Victoria bother his feelings, like I do.

"Halloween isn't for a few more weeks," Victoria reminds us. "Hey, Quinny, too bad you missed the field trip yesterday. You wouldn't believe how many dogs were at the shelter, including the cutest puppy I've ever seen. I'm probably going to adopt it."

"What?"

"But I can't decide between a puppy or a kitten."

"Lucky duck!"

"Maybe I'll get one of each. Or an Angora rabbit. Too bad your sister is allergic."

Then Victoria smiles, like she is so happy she isn't me. How can a person be such big buckets of mean with one single smile? *Grrrrr.* I adjust my bandanna again. If I were a real pirate with a real hook, Victoria's life would be in danger, that's for sure.

After morning meeting, we go back to our desks and Ms. Yoon starts talking about our *how-to* writing assignment again. It's time for us to turn in our topics.

"But first let's each share with the class the topics we've chosen. It will whet our appetites for the final pieces, which we'll celebrate at our publishing party next month."

Ms. Yoon calls on people, starting from the left side of the room. And everybody stands up and says the title of their *how-to* topic. Some of the topics are fun, like when Caleb stands up and says he's doing *How to Stand on Your Head Without Falling Over*. Some are dull, like when Kaylee says she's doing *How to Make French Braids*. Bor-ing.

When it's Victoria's turn, she stands up and says, "My topic is *How to Raise Chickens in Your Backyard—and Start a Business Selling Eggs*."

And I just sit there, frozen. Because that is my *how-to* topic, too. I told Victoria about it earlier this week. I was so happy to figure out a topic that wouldn't hurt Piper's feelings.

"Quinny? Quinny . . . your turn. Would you like to share your topic?"

I look at Ms. Yoon and a lump bumps up in my throat. I don't want to seem like a copycat. That's what people will think if I say the same thing as Victoria.

"I need more time," I whisper. "I'm sorry, Ms. Yoon. I don't have a topic ready. Can I have just one more day? I'm really sorry."

Ms. Yoon looks disappointed, but nods. "Let's move along, then. Alex?"

I don't even hear what Alex says because my head feels swollen with shock about what Victoria just did. Those chickens were *my* topic. And she knew it.

Science is next, and Ms. Yoon hands out a sheet called MONARCH BUTTERFLIES: BEAUTIFUL BUT POISONOUS. She talks about how those butterflies are born, how they grow and live. How birds know not to eat them because they're filled with poison. Even baby birds know.

She asks questions and people raise their hands, but my head still feels swollen with shock, so I just stare down at my sheet. Then I grab my pencil, and by the BEAUTIFUL BUT POISONOUS part, I write, *JUST LIKE VICTORIA.*

I trace my words, over and over, until they're the darkest ones on the page. This feels good, like I'm telling the truth. We're supposed to tell the truth in life, aren't we?

But then a wave of guilty yuck ruins that truthy feeling, and I'm not so sure.

I flip my pencil around and erase what I wrote, super quick, so no one sees it.

At recess, my courage finally grows bigger than my shock. Victoria can't just steal my *how-to* topic and get away with it. I decide to walk over to her and stand up for myself.

But when I do, she is already in the middle of talking to a bunch of other girls and won't let me interrupt her. So I poke her, very politely.

"Excuse me, Victoria, but why did you steal my chickens?"

Victoria ignores me and keeps talking to the others.

"Excuse me again, Victoria, but you don't even

know how to take care of my chickens. Plus I told you I was doing them as a topic *first*."

She turns to me. "The chickens live at my aunt's house. They're *my* family chickens."

"But I'm the one who takes care of them!"

"Look, I don't have time for this," snaps Victoria. "I've got a party to plan—"

"A party?" I perk up a little. I love parties.

"If you're done being rude, I was going to tell you all about it. It's an animal costume party, to raise money for the animal shelter, and it's on Sunday, October twenty-fourth, in three weeks."

Three weeks? Sunday afternoon? That's the same time as Hopper's birthday. And I already got tickets to go with him to the Brain Expo in New York City. Victoria can't have her animal costume party at the exact same time.

"Victoria, wait, I really need to talk to you."

"We're making the guest list. And planning the invitations and food and decorations. We're asking guests to donate pet food or supplies or money for the shelter. I might even let people bring their own pets to the party, too."

I can't take it anymore. Victoria stole my *how-to* idea without even saying sorry. And now she's planning an amazing party I can't go to. Even if I could go, I don't have a pet to take. And that's too many sour things happening all at once. Where is Hopper when I need him? Why did he have to pick today to have his tonsils out? I wait until the yard guard isn't looking, and then I sneak back inside the building and run to my classroom.

That's where Ms. Yoon eats her lunch while we're at recess. Sometimes she lets me hang out with her. I only ask if I'm really, truly, absolutely desperate. Like today.

"Ms. Yoon?"

She usually sits at her desk eating a sandwich, but someone else is there now. I gasp—it's that other yard-guard lady from recess last week, the mean one who said I tripped Victoria when I really didn't. Then she tattled on me to Ms. Yoon. I don't know her name.

"I'm . . . sorry. I was just looking for my teacher?"

The yard-guard lady puts down her fork

and makes a chilly, impatient face. She has the straightest part in her hair and the straightest posture in her back that I've ever seen.

"Her name is Ms. Yoon. Do you know where she went?"

"Ms. Yoon is gone. I've been assigned to substitute for her."

"But she was just here a minute ago. What happened? When is she coming back?"

"I have no idea when she's coming back. When or if, for that matter."

"What do you mean, *if*?"

"Do you have a hall pass, young lady?"

"Where did Ms. Yoon go? Please, I need to talk to her."

"You can't just wander the halls without permission."

"Is she mad about all the lice? Is that baby in her belly okay? Did she quit her job because she just can't take it anymore?"

"Ms. Yoon's personal circumstances are her own business. Now, please go back to where you belong, and don't let me catch you wandering without a hall pass again."

"Yes, ma'am."

I run to ask Nurse Mira—she'll know where Ms. Yoon is. She knows everything.

On the way, I get lucky. Principal Ramsey walks by. "Principal Ramsey! You're just the person I was looking for! I have some terrible news—Ms. Yoon is gone!"

"Quinny, hello there. Aren't you supposed to be at recess?"

"Please tell her to come back! I promise not to talk or wiggle or bicker with Victoria. I promise not to bother her at lunch if she wants to eat her sandwich in peace! Can you tell her? Maybe you should write this down so you don't forget? My parents are always forgetting things. Or I can type it for you. I know how to type now. Hopper is teaching me—"

"Quinny, please calm your engine down—"

"That's exactly why I wanted to go find Ms. Yoon. She helps me do that!"

"When there's news to share about Ms. Yoon, believe me, you'll be the first to hear."

"Okay, but did you know that substitute lady sitting in Ms. Yoon's chair is very cranky? Isn't there another one you can find who likes children in the first place?"

"Quinny, I'm afraid I can't take requests for substitute teachers. Try your best to get along with whoever is in charge. Give them a chance and make good choices, okay?"

"Okay, but—"

"Ah-ah—no *but*s."

"I mean, yes, Principal Ramsey, okay."

After recess, the substitute tells us that her name is Mrs. Flavio and she used to teach math to middle schoolers. She looks at us with very strict eyes and says we're all going to get along fine as long as we can follow *a few simple rules*.

For example: Raise your hand and wait to be called on before speaking, keep your hands to yourself, respect other people's personal space, keep your desk neat and orderly, no running in class, no chatting. No doing anything interesting at all, I guess.

Then Mrs. Flavio calls out our names from Ms. Yoon's official teacher book so she can figure out who we are. When she gets to me, she calls out "Eleanor Quinston Bumble."

"That's me!" I wave both my hands. "But my real name is Quinny."

"Well, it says *Eleanor* right here." She blows a loud breath and scribbles something.

When Mrs. Flavio gets to Victoria, she calls out "Victoria Rose Porridge," and Victoria sits up straight and raises her hand and says "present" in this perfect little voice that matches her perfect pink name. And Mrs. Flavio gives her a look, like *Maybe the world isn't such a horrible place with lovely proper children like you in it.*

After she runs out of names to call, Mrs. Flavio hands out work sheets for cursive.

But when I pull out my crayons to color the dancing aardvark at the top of my sheet, she says, "Put your crayons away. It's time to practice cursive."

"Ms. Yoon always lets me color in the animals on my cursive sheet."

"Well, I'm in charge now, and there's no coloring in cursive. Put away your crayons."

I think *Put away your crayons* must be the

saddest sentence in the whole English language. But I obey that sad, sad sentence.

Victoria leans over and whispers to me, "Coloring is for babies."

But Mrs. Flavio doesn't even hear that mean whisper! She just looks past me and compliments Victoria's cursive, even though mine is just as neat (well, almost).

Later, she calls on Victoria to take a note to the main office, even though my hand is stretching higher and waving ten times faster.

She orders Alex to settle down and focus on his work.

She reminds Xander to keep his hands to himself.

She tells me to stop wiggling and chatting.

I am trying so hard not to wiggle and chat. I am trying so so sooooooo hard to give Mrs. Flavio a chance, like Principal Ramsey said. But she is not giving *me* a chance.

She snaps at me to push my chair in as she walks by my table. Then she snaps that all four legs of my chair have to be on the floor at all times, which means I can't rock back and forth, which helps me to calm my engine down.

She even picks on my reading log when I turn it in because I've been reading other things this week instead of a *book* book.

"Is this some kind of joke? You read a vacuum cleaner manual? And billboards?"

"It was a really cool vacuum cleaner," I inform her. "It even vacuums upside down. And the manual was in three languages! Plus I read billboards in the car on the way to visit my cousins. Ms. Yoon doesn't care what we read as long as it's words, and twenty minutes a day."

"Well, I'm in charge now. From now on, please read an actual book."

Later, during math, she shushes me when I lean over to ask Silas what his favorite kind of cupcake is. And also when I turn around to share a cupcake doodle with Amanda. I point out to Mrs. Flavio that there's a word problem on my sheet that's *about* cupcakes, which is what made me think of cupcakes. She shushes me for pointing that out, too.

Dessert in your lunch = delicious.

Dessert in your math = distracting.

Basically, Mrs. Flavio hates it when I talk, or move, or scratch an itch. She wants straight, silent rows of frozen robot children.

I don't stand a chance.

During social studies, our last subject of the day, she says, "Eleanor, if I catch you chatting one more time, you'll get recess detention. Is that clear?"

Recess detention is when you lose recess. It's serious stuff. Ms. Yoon never even does that. But I can tell Mrs. Flavio really means it, so I bite my tongue to keep it quiet. I sit on my hands to keep them still. I scrunch my eyes shut to keep my personality from showing. (Which is really hard. I don't know how Hopper does it!)

But a few minutes later, Mrs. Flavio catches me chatting again. And *boom*, she takes away my recess. For Monday and Tuesday, too. "But, Mrs. Flavio, that's not fair," I say. "I didn't chat two more times, so why are you taking away *two* recesses?"

She looks startled that I'm actually having a conversation with her.

"Plus did you know Ms. Yoon never takes away recess, not even from the real baddies? She puts them on a private island, or she gives them an errand to run—"

"Eleanor, that's enough!"

"She never yells, either, by the way. She whispers, and then we all quiet down to hear what she's saying—you may want to give that a try."

Mrs. Flavio's lips press together into a line as straight as the part in her hair. Then her voice booms, "Not one more word, Eleanor—do you hear me? Not one single word!"

Everyone stares at me. Victoria snickers a smile. *My name is Quinny*, I don't say, since that would be four more words. I bite my tongue and sit there, without Ms. Yoon, without Hopper. Without my precious recess for two whole days. It feels like I'm trapped in a cage and that meanie sub just threw away the key.

Mrs. Meanie Sub. That's her new name.

Seven

Hopper

The world is dark and blurry. It gets lighter. It tilts and wobbles.

"Hopper, sweetheart . . ."

My eyes open some more. Everything feels crooked. Where am I?

"Hopper, it's Mommy. We're all done—your tonsils are out."

And then I remember: I'm at the hospital. I had an operation.

I am still alive. But I don't feel so great. There's a gentle hand on my back. A bucket at my chin. I throw up into it.

Mom wipes my mouth and hugs me. Dad is here, and Ty and Trevor, too. Everyone hugs me.

Gently, all at once, and for a long time. Dad never cries, but he has tears in his eyes now. This kind of hugging never happens at home.

"Why is everyone here?" I try to say, but most of the sentence doesn't come out.

"*Shhhh,*" Mom says. "Remember, Dr. Merkle

said your throat will be a bit sore afterward. The twins left school early to come here. And Dad didn't go to work at all."

"Why?"

"What a silly question, Hopper—because we love you. We love you so very much."

But I'm not used to feeling so important. I start crying and it feels like going down a slide— it's hard to stop once you start.

Then I notice a long, thin tube sticking out of my arm. That must be the IV that Dr. Parva told me about. It doesn't hurt, but I don't like it, so I try to pull it out.

"Whoa, there," says Nurse Chuck, who's suddenly back. "Gotta keep that in a little while longer, buddy."

Dr. Merkle comes in.

"Job well done, Hopper," he says. "That wasn't so bad, was it?"

It wasn't so fantastic, either. He says I have to rest now because the medicine they used to make me sleep during the operation is wearing off, and that's why my stomach feels weird and my head is groggy. I don't even care about Popsicles or ice cream.

A few minutes later, I'm crying again.

"Hopper, oh, sweetie." Mom hugs me again. "What's wrong?"

I don't know. The operation is over. I woke up, like Dr. Parva said. I did a good job, like Dr. Merkle said. My whole family is here and they love me.

Maybe I'm crying because it's over. I was trying so hard not to be scared. I held it all in. But now it all comes out, right into Mom's arms.

After I'm empty, I close my eyes. I just want to sleep.

On the way home, my brothers sit on both sides of me, in the back of the minivan. No one pounds or pushes me. I lean on a shoulder, then another shoulder. They put my blanket over me gently. I wish I felt like this with Trevor and Ty more often.

The van stops, and Dad carries me inside and upstairs to my bed. My very own comfy bed. I wrap my arms around him so I don't fall. He puts me down slowly.

I try to sleep, but my stomach is still not happy. There's a weird taste in my mouth. Did I eat something weird in my sleep? My head still feels funny, too. I don't want anyone to bother me. I need some water. I'm not thirsty at all. I feel like gagging.

I want Mom to sit on the edge of my bed and rub my back. I want her to go away.

I don't know what I want.

"It's okay, honey," she says. "You'll start to feel better soon. And then, Popsicles!"

I wish *soon* meant *right now*. Having my tonsils out was supposed to make me feel better, but it actually made me feel worse. I feel worse now than I've ever felt in my whole life. I wonder if Dr. Merkle made a giant mistake.

Eight

Quinny

"Hopper, Hopper, Hopper!"

I see his dad carrying him into his house, so I run as fast as I can from the bus stop. But, *phooey*—the edge of his blanket disappears through his front door before I get there.

"Hopper, come back out here." I knock on his door. "How are your tonsils? Did they get 'em all out? I had a really bad day. How are you? Did you know Ms. Yoon is gone and now we have a grumpy sub who hates my crayons, and, by the way, how was the hospital? I made you a card, plus a word search full of ice-cream flavors!"

Hopper's mom comes out and smiles at me, all patient.

"Quinny, Hopper needs to sleep—he's still a little woozy from the operation."

But he slept during his operation, so I don't see why he needs to sleep more now. "Mrs. Grey, I'm really good at perking Hopper up. Just give me five minutes—I promise he'll feel better."

"Honey, as soon as he's able to play, we'll let you know."

"But I made him a word search—"

"That's great, but he needs to rest now. And I need you to respect that, okay?"

Okay, fine, I can take a hint.

Piper is away on a playdate and Cleo is still napping, so I'll just go find something else to do. I'm sure those chickens would be thrilled to see me, for example.

A soccer ball flies past my head as I walk over to Mrs. Porridge's house.

"Hey, watch it!" I yell as the bully twins come running after the ball. I run after it, too, and I catch up with it and kick it. I run and kick and run and kick, and the boys are about to catch up to me and steal that ball away when I KICK IT FOR REAL, and the ball goes flying . . . up, up,

and away! Over our heads and through the sky and through the trees . . .

And then—*poof*—it's gone.

"Holy moly," grunts Trevor/Ty.

"Are you bionic?" snarls Ty/Trevor.

"As you know, kicking is one of my strengths," I inform them, and then I run after that ball before they can get to it first.

Nine

Hopper

My throat hurts.

Mom offers me a Popsicle. Some water. A back rub.

Nothing really works.

Not even pistachio ice cream, my favorite.

I think Dr. Merkle definitely made a mistake taking out my tonsils. A huge mistake.

"Hopper, sweetie, try to sleep," says Mom.

I'm sleepy, but I can't fall asleep.

There's noise from outside. Light leaks in through my closed window shade. I roll over and pull at the shade to peek out, and I realize I must already be asleep.

Because Quinny would never be out there, kicking a soccer ball with my brothers, in real life. Never in a million years.

I must be dreaming.

Ten
Quinny

I race those bully twins for that soccer ball! I twist around trees, hop a giant rock, and dodge some lawn chairs. I zoom as fast as I can, but still they get to the ball first.

But then they freeze. And back up slowly, their eyes huge with fear.

Disco and Cha-Cha are hopping toward them now, flapping and *brrrr*-ing.

Those bully twins are shaking. Because Disco and Cha-Cha's mother (whose name is Freya, but that's another story) used to live around here, and she once attacked those twins so bad that they're scared of all chickens now.

Even these two scrawny, mini ones, who don't even know how to lay eggs yet.

"*Brrrrip,*" says Disco, tilting a tiny beady eye. "*SCREEEE-bup.*"

"*Bip buup,*" says Cha-Cha, shaking her baldish feathery bottom.

The twins scoop up their soccer ball and run for their lives.

"How'd you girls escape?" I ask the chickens. "C'mon, let's get you back home."

"*Sssssss!*" hisses Walter the cat, who I didn't even know was here, too.

"Oh, hello, Walter. Calm down. I won't hurt Cha-Cha. I know she's your favorite."

Disco screeches at Walter to calm down, too. Walter screeches at Disco to mind her own business. Cha-Cha just stands there, all innocent and scruffy, balancing on her bony dinosaur-starfish feet. "*Errp,*" she says. "*Oop.*"

"Sorry, I don't have a treat," I tell her. "Let's go home and find you some raisins."

"*Oooh prrrr.*" Cha-Cha jumps onto Walter's back, and he walks her home.

Disco follows them, *woop*-ing and *wrrr*-ing and *SCREEEEEE*-ing, flapping her dusty feathers. I know an upset chicken when I see one. "It's okay, Disco. You'll get raisins, too."

We walk to Mrs. Porridge's yard, which is noisy with hammering and arguing. Hopper's Grandpa Gooley, who doesn't even live here, by the way, is nailing wood pieces together into a rectangle shape on the ground. Mrs. Porridge is standing over him with a sour face and her hands on her hips.

She is telling him to stop. He is telling her to stop telling him to stop.

"Grandpa Gooley, why are you and Mrs. Porridge arguing?"

"We're not arguing. We're debating, like civilized human beings. Right, Myrna?"

"Hmmmpt," says Mrs. Porridge.

"My point is, that's not much of a chicken coop." Grandpa Gooley points toward the rickety shed that Mrs. Porridge wants to use for Disco and Cha-Cha once they outgrow the screened-in porch coop. She already fenced in a little outdoor run for them by the shed.

"The shed is fine—those chickens don't need a palace," she snaps.

"That skimpy poultry netting you used for the run won't protect them from predators," says Grandpa Gooley. "And the shed is too small, with poor ventilation."

"Quinny and I are perfectly capable of taking care of these chickens without a know-it-all man swooping in to save the day," says Mrs. Porridge.

"I'm not swooping, just trying to help," he says.

"Quinny, the *chalet des poulets* is officially under construction. I've got some extra work gloves if you'd like to lend a hand."

"Absolutely, Grandpa Gooley! But why did you just call it the shah-lay de poo-lay? Is it because chickens *poo* a lot, and also *lay* eggs?"

"*Chalet* is another word for 'house,' and *poulets* means 'chickens' in French," he says. "But I like your explanation better."

He hands me some work gloves, and I bring him more pieces of wood, which he nails together to make the bottom frame of the coop. He says I'm such a good helper I can help him again tomorrow if I want.

"I'll show you how to hammer a nail," he says. "How's my grandson doing? They weren't home when I stopped by earlier."

"Oh, Grandpa Gooley, it's so sad. I haven't seen Hopper since yesterday! I mean, I saw his foot when they carried him inside just now, but his mom wouldn't let me in."

"Imagine that."

"I've really had the bad-luckiest day ever."

"Sorry to hear that, Quinny."

"I'm not even kidding—it was the worst. Hopper wasn't in school, and now he's busy sleeping. And Victoria made fun of my lice bandanna and stole my chickens, AND she's planning an animal costume party I can't go to. Plus, did I mention that my precious teacher Ms. Yoon is gone and Mrs. Meanie Sub hates me?"

"Sounds like you're feeling mighty low."

"What did my grand-niece do this time?" Mrs. Porridge sighs. She's walking back over to us with a tray of minty lemonade, which is my favorite, except for the mint.

"Oh, Mrs. Porridge, I know you love her and I don't want to tattle, but I told her I was going to write about taking care of the chickens for an assignment, and then Victoria stole that idea for herself without even telling me. I can't take it anymore. She's so awful I wish she would switch schools."

"That's a pretty extreme thing to say, Quinny," says Grandpa Gooley. "Is it that bad?"

Part of me wants to tell Grandpa Gooley what Victoria is really like. The stares; the snappy, hurtful comments; the bossiness.

But then I look at Mrs. Porridge's sad face, and I feel bad for complaining. Victoria's not *all* bad. She leaves me stickers at my locker. She gives me candy and braids my hair. She gives me fashion advice. (I usually ignore it, but still, it's nice of her.)

"I'm sorry, Mrs. Porridge. I know it's not nice to say not-nice things about people, even if they're not-nice in the first place. I didn't mean to tattle on your pretty grand-niece."

"Please don't give up on her, Quinny. Victoria needs some extra help to do the right thing sometimes. She could use more friends like you."

"You really think I can help her be nicer?"

"I do."

"But, before, you said, 'We are what we are— no amount of conversation's going to change that.'"

Mrs. Porridge does an almost-smile now. (She almost never does a full smile. I've only seen it once.) "Well, before, I was talking about chickens. People are usually more complicated than chickens. There's good and bad mixed up together in all of us."

I promise Mrs. Porridge I won't give up on Victoria. Not yet, at least.

In exchange, I make her promise to let Grandpa Gooley come back and finish building the *chalet des poulets.*

"Deal." She holds out her hand and we shake.

I'm getting pretty good at this negotiating thing.

The phone rings in the house, and Mrs. Porridge goes to answer it. She comes back a minute later. "Quinny, your parents want you back home. It seems they need to talk to you."

"About what?"

"I'm just guessing here, but sounds like it's probably none of my business."

My stomach twists. I think I know what, but I hope I'm wrong.

"Quinny, have a seat." Mom and Daddy sit on the sofa, all calm and serious.

"What is it? Did the school call? It's not my fault, honest. That meanie sub hates me—"

"No, the school didn't call," says Daddy. "But maybe we should call the school . . . ?"

"No! Not at all! That would be a big waste of time, and I know how busy you guys are! Let's just move right along, shall we?"

"Okay, well, we wanted to talk to you alone, while Piper isn't here," says Mom. "We have an idea for how our family can help with Piper's bed-wetting, and it involves you."

"Me? Why me?"

"Well, it was kind of your idea in the first place. You inspired us to do a little research."

"I did? What are you talking about?"

Then my parents tell me the idea. And it's the worst idea I have ever heard. (Even though I had the same idea for my first *how-to* topic.) It turns out there really is an alarm to help stop kids from peeing in their beds at night. My parents got one and they want to clip it onto Piper's pajamas, and then it will beep very loud if she has an accident, but that beeping would also wake up Cleo, which is not great because my parents already spent a really long time trying to get that baby to sleep through the night in her crib.

"So we'd like you to move into Piper and Cleo's room—just for a couple of weeks—and let Piper sleep in your room so she can try out this alarm without waking anyone up."

"But she'll touch all my things! She'll pee in my bed!"

"We'll put a liner on the bed," says Daddy.

"Two liners," adds Mom.

I don't care. It's still gross. Someone else's pee is always worse than your own pee.

"How come Piper can do my third-grade math, but she can't figure out how to go to the bathroom at night?"

"Bed-wetting is a phase some kids go through as they grow up," says Mom. "We love Piper, and we want to try to help her get a better night's sleep. Will you help us?"

Grrrr. It's not my problem that Piper has a small bladder. But now I guess it is, since I'm being kicked out of my own room because of her. I don't mind sharing a room with Cleo—I actually like that baby sister since she doesn't try to lick me, like certain other sisters do. I just don't want Piper touching my stuff with her booty cooties. And she will. She's a stinky little sneak who gets away with everything.

"Okay," I grumble. "But what if that alarm thing doesn't even work?"

"It may not. If it doesn't help her start waking up to use the toilet, we'll try something else. The room switch is temporary, Quinny. We appreciate your flexibility."

I didn't think life could get any worse after what happened at school today. But I was wrong. Pee-U Piper will now be peeing in *my* bed at night. And touching all *my* things, which are none of her business. The worst thing of all: How will I see into Hopper's room from Cleo and Piper's room? It's all the way on the other side of the house!

Eleven
Hopper

I'm supposed to be sleeping. But I feel fidgety and sore, and my eyes keep popping open. I roll over and peek out the window again.

It's dark outside, but there's a lamp on in Quinny's bedroom.

And there's Piper, jumping up and down on Quinny's bed.

She's wearing Quinny's boots and Quinny's sun hat.

She's spinning Quinny's favorite stuffed monkey around by one leg.

What?

Piper does the splits as she jumps, and one of

the boots flies off her foot and hits the window. Then I hear a rooster crowing.

I must still be asleep, I guess. This is one long, strange dream.

Twelve

Quinny

Cleo is so excited that I'm sleeping in her room that she won't go to sleep.

It takes an hour to get that baby down.

Then she wakes back up and tries to climb out of her crib. Twice.

Luckily, her crib has room for both of us in it, if I bend my knees. Problem solved. Except . . . the sound of Cleo sucking her Binky is really annoying when it's next to your ear.

Finally, everything gets quiet.

That's when Piper's bed-wetting alarm beeps all the way down the hall and wakes everybody up. Because, surprise: that beep isn't just loud— it's very, very, extra-very loud. I can hear Piper crying now, and Mom yelling at Daddy that he should have turned down the volume on that alarm before attaching it to Piper's pj's. Then Daddy yells at Mom that he thought *she'd* done that. Then Cleo spits out her Binky and starts crying, too.

This bedroom-switching experiment is officially a disaster, if you ask me.

I pick Cleo up and go out into the hall. Her cries quiet into whimpers, and she grabs my hair. I walk her over to my old room. I peek inside.

And then a volcano bursts up in my belly.

Because all my stuff is where I *didn't* leave it. My twit-ster's booty cooties are everywhere. She even moved stuff on my bulletin board! I'm holding Cleo, so I can't give Piper a consequence for her bad behavior, but believe me, I will. Oh, I will. Just as soon as we're alone and nobody's looking.

For now, I just yell. Then Mom and Daddy yell at me to stop yelling. And I yell at them to stop yelling. But here's what I discovered: yelling at a person to stop yelling doesn't actually stop them from doing it. It just makes the baby you're holding cry some more.

After we're all out of yelling and crying, I take Cleo back to our room. I'm too mad to sleep, but I lie there, trying to get her to close her eyes. And it works, for a few precious minutes of sleepy silence. Long enough for my body to feel softer and my head to go quiet.

But then Disco starts up with his cock-a-doodle-do, which really should be spelled *SCREEEE-KOOOOR-SCREEEE* because that's what it actually sounds like. And Cleo starts wiggling again and playing with my hair. It's getting light out now. It's no use. We're up.

I stub my toe in the hall as I step around a pile of stinky sheets on my way to the bathroom. Between all the crying, peeing, snoring, and yelling, I did not get a good night's sleep. Neither did my parents, I guess, because no one remembers to feed me breakfast.

Luckily, I know where everything is. It only takes me a couple of minutes to fill my tummy with Cheerios (and cookies), and then I head outside to do my chicken chores.

I walk through my yard toward Mrs. Porridge's house. The air is calmer and cooler out here. Maybe

I'll pitch a tent and sleep in the yard tonight. It's a lot more peaceful outside than it is in the house.

But then, on my way to the chickens, I hear a scream. It's coming from the direction of Mrs. Porridge's house, only it doesn't sound like Disco or Cha-Cha.

That's a human person I hear screaming now.

Thirteen
Hopper

The screaming is what finally wakes me up.

It sounds like an opera singer falling off a cliff.

I look out the window and see Quinny running through my yard, toward Mrs. Porridge's house. She's running toward all the screaming.

I rub at my face, but this is no dream. I push up from my bed and find my balance. . . . *Whoa.* I pull a sweatshirt on over my pajamas. I forget about my sore throat and my woozy head. I go downstairs and sneak outside and start after Quinny, through the trees.

But then a voice comes at me from behind.

"Hopper? Sweetie, just where do you think you're going?"

I turn around, maybe too fast, and that's when the world starts to spin.

Fourteen

Quinny

Who knew Victoria Porridge could scream so loud? She's on the floor of the chicken porch, flailing her hands and feet in the air. "My hands! My hands!"

Mrs. Porridge is there, too, and looks annoyed. "Pull yourself together, Victoria. I expect more from the president of her own fashion empire."

"You didn't tell me there'd be poop!"

"Of course there's poop. Where do you think chickens do their business? Right where they're standing. There's no magic invisible chicken toilet that cleans itself."

"Ooop," says Cha-Cha, bopping around on her giant starfish feet. Walter slinks over and rubs

against her. Then Cha-Cha jumps onto Walter for another kitty-back ride.

"Brrrrup." Disco skitters over and slaps her wings at Walter, who hisses at her.

Victoria hiccups and looks at her poopy hands, like she wishes someone would get rid of them for her.

"Victoria, it's okay, just go wash your hands," I tell her. "But hey, what are you doing here in the first place?"

"I invited her," says Mrs. Porridge. "Since my grand-niece is writing about how to take care of chickens, I thought she should take care of some. And who better to teach her than the person already taking care of them so well?"

Mrs. Porridge stares at me. I stare back at her.

"I'm talking about you, Quinny."

"Oh, right!"

"Now, could you please show Victoria what taking care of chickens is all about?"

"Sure, but I think she needs a wet wipe first."

"My shoes," whimpers Victoria. Her ballet flats are stuck in the chicken muck.

"I told you to wear your rubber boots." Mrs. Porridge throws Victoria a wipe.

"But it wasn't raining."

"Well, don't forget them tomorrow."

"Tomorrow?"

"Yes, tomorrow," Ms. Porridge snaps. "These young chickens need to be fed, watered, and cared for daily, of course."

"Great," Victoria mutters, picking up a ballet flat from the muck.

"It's not as much work as it sounds," I tell her. "Just follow what I do. First we clean the poop out of their feeder."

"They poop in their food?"

"They don't realize they're doing it. So we clean it out and add fresh starter feed. And they need fresh water daily, too—that's super important since chickens get thirsty really fast. And then, once a week, we clean out the mini-henhouse . . . with this."

I show Victoria the trowel and I push open the door to the big cardboard box that we use as Disco and Cha-Cha's mini-henhouse. They even have a mini-roost and a mini–nest box in there, since I figured they are in training to be real grown-up chickens one day.

Victoria coughs. "Why is it so dusty in there? And where are all the eggs?"

"They won't lay eggs until they're older. Gee, Victoria, you really don't know much about chickens, do you?"

"I know that the fancy brown eggs at the super-market sell for five dollars and sixty cents a dozen. If these chickens would lay some eggs instead of making dust and poop, I could make some money."

I can't believe she just said that. They're not even her chickens.

"Why are their feathers so clumpy?" she asks. "They look all bony and sick."

"They're teenagers. They're still growing their grown-up feathers. Now, can you please pay attention?" I hand Victoria the trowel. "So to clean the henhouse, you scrape out all the old bedding and put it in this bin over here, for compost."

"Ewww."

"It's not that bad, you can wear work gloves.

Then we add clean bedding from that hay bale over in the corner. And then . . . my favorite part, we feed them treats from here."

I walk Victoria over to the metal can of kitchen-scrap treats. She wrinkles her nose when I open it. "You mean those chickens eat garbage?"

"They're kitchen scraps. Just leftover food mixed together. Anything except citrus, onions, or fish. You'll get used to the smell. We keep it in a metal can so mice don't get into it."

"Mice?"

Victoria looks queasy. I feel a little bit bad for her. But mostly, seeing her slimed by chicken poop puts me in an excellent mood. And a good mood is like a bad cold—it's easy for people to catch it from you if you're in the same place together. So after she leaves, I run over to Hopper's bedroom window so he can catch my good mood from me.

"Hopper, Hopper, Hopper! Wait till you hear about Victoria and the chicken poop!"

No answer. I throw a pebble up at his window, just a tiny one. Still no answer.

So I go around to his front door. His mom says he's still resting. She thanks me for respecting that, again. "But, Mrs. Grey! Victoria got slimed by chicken poop. You should have seen her face. I need to tell Hopper. Also, I need to give him the stuff I made—"

"I can make sure he gets it, Quinny."

"Can't I just come in and hand it to him? I promise I won't say a word."

"Maybe later this afternoon. We'll see how he's feeling."

Maybe later = Probably never.

On my way home, I see the bully twins wearing their soccer stuff and getting in their van.

"Hey, Big Mouth," says one of their heads, looking at me. "Come with us."

"Yeah, come watch the game," says the other head. "You can meet our coach."

Their father, who's in the driver's seat, nods like it's okay with him and says I can run home to ask. I'm tempted for a second. But then I look up at Hopper's window.

"No thanks," I tell those two talking heads. "I'm waiting for Hopper to finish resting."

"We're gonna cream Riverdale. You don't want to miss it."

"They won't know what hit 'em. It's gonna be a bloodbath."

Hmmm . . . I don't know what a bloodbath is, but it does not sound boring. I run home and find Daddy, and he says yes, so I run back and jump in the van and go to my very first soccer game of all time.

Fifteen

Hopper

Saturday afternoon Quinny comes to see me. She brings balloons, a get-well card, and an ice-cream word search.

"Sorry they didn't have tonsil-shaped balloons," she says. "But I put *PISTACHIO* in the word search twice, because I know it's your favorite flavor. Now, tell me everything!"

"My throat," I whisper.

"Oh, I forgot you're not supposed to talk. So just tell me the important parts. Like about your tonsils and the hospital! And when are you coming back to school? Because Victoria is being awful, and Ms. Yoon is gone and we have a meanie sub—"

"Ms. Yoon is gone?"

"She disappeared! But don't worry. Principal Ramsey said I'll be the first to know when they figure out what happened. Now, tell me all about the hospital!"

I don't want to talk about the hospital. I tell her about my weird dreams instead.

"You weren't dreaming," Quinny says. "I really did play soccer with the twins. They even forced me to go to a soccer game with them, while you were sleeping."

"They forced you?"

"Yeah, well, sort of . . . It's a long story."

But then she doesn't tell the story. She acts quiet, like she's hiding something.

Quinny's never usually quiet. "Quinny, what's wrong?"

"Nothing. Oh! By the way, also, Piper really *was* in my room last night, going bananas. You didn't dream that, either. We had to switch rooms 'cause my parents said so."

That's a bummer. I'm used to having Quinny's room right across from my bedroom window. I guess I missed a lot over the last couple of days.

"Why did they make you switch rooms?"

"That's Piper's personal business and I'm not allowed to talk about it, even though Mom says there's nothing to be embarrassed about since a lot of kids wet their beds."

Then Quinny turns red and says, "Oops! Can you forget I mentioned that part?"

"No problem."

"Anyway, I'm so glad your mom finally let me see you. Now, show me those tonsils! Where are they? Did they measure them? Will you make it into the world-record book?"

"I didn't get to keep my tonsils."

"What? Why not?"

"I just didn't."

"But they belong to you! Like a tooth or a scab—they ARE you."

I shrug. She's right, in a way.

"You should get to take them home from the hospital. And shellac them, like in art class, or keep them in a jar, along with all your other body parts, on the shelf."

"Quinny, none of those are real. They're just anatomy models."

"I know that, silly. But that's what makes your

111

tonsils so special! Why should the hospital get to keep all the good stuff?"

"I'm pretty sure they just threw them away."

"No! I bet they're in the lost and found. . . . Hey, let's go check! I'm free right now."

"Why would I want them back? What could I do with leftover tonsils?"

Quinny looks at me and then snorts. "Are you kidding? A ton of stuff! Like . . . I don't know. You could scare away bullies. Or invent a new game for gym called tonsil ball."

"Yeah, right."

"You could put them in Victoria's lunch box for a slimy Halloween surprise. Or offer the chickens a really, really unique snack!"

That's disgusting. I try not to laugh.

"Wait, I know! You could erupt a tonsil-cano at the school science fair!" she says. "Or you could hang them from your minivan's rearview mirror."

"Like slimy dice?" I laugh.

Mom comes in to make sure everything is okay. It is. She smiles and goes away.

"You could surprise your mom with two-of-a-kind earrings for her birthday," says Quinny,

rolling over and giggling, and pulling me down
with her. *"Eeeeewwwww."*

Laughing hurts, but it also helps me feel better. Being with Quinny helps, too.

"Thanks," I whisper.

"For what?"

"You always know how to cheer me up."

Quinny's face beams. "You're right. Hopper . . .
Oh, wow, that's it! That's it!"

I don't get what she's saying.

"You just solved the biggest problem of my life! Oh, thank you!"

She throws a hug onto me, rougher than she's supposed to, and then runs off.

A second later, her head pops back into my doorway. "Wait here! I'll be right back!"

Sixteen

Quinny

How to Cheer Up a Friend
By Quinny (not Eleanor) Bumble

1) If your friend is sick, make a cheery get-well card and go visit him, ASAP.
2) Bring Popsicles, his favorite ice cream, or a special treat, like cheese and crackers.
3) Tell a joke to make him laugh. If the first one doesn't work, keep trying.
4) Drag your friend to a chicken dance party! I suggest any song by the Beatles.
5) A whoopee cushion is another good idea, but make sure it isn't broken first.
6) If your friend is extra sad, do something

115

silly, like a fishy face or crossed eyes so he forgets his blues.

7) SMILE and be in a good mood—because Ms. Yoon said a good mood is contagious, which means you can catch it from other people like a barfy stomach bug!

I run back to Hopper's room. "It's just a rough draft so far, but what do you think?"

Hopper looks at it for a moment. His serious face doesn't change.

"I thought you were going to write about how to raise chickens," he says.

"Oh, I was! But then Victoria stole that topic. But she can't steal this one, because she has no idea how to cheer up a friend! What about you? Did you think of a topic yet?"

"Probably how to juggle. Ms. Yoon is giving me extra time because of my operation."

"Hmmm . . . you're the best juggler, Hopper. That's true. But . . ."

"But what?"

"Maybe you can think even bigger."

Seventeen

Hopper

Think bigger? I don't know what Quinny means.

Not at first.

But then I think about the last couple of days. I look over at my favorite book, on the floor by my bed: Frank H. Netter's *Atlas of Human Anatomy.* It has just a few pictures of tonsils in it. When I was having my tonsillectomy, I wanted to see more. And learn more. I wanted to know everything.

I get out my charcoal pencils and my sketchbook. I write at the top of a page:

How to Have Your Tonsils Out

I show Quinny. She picks up a pencil and changes it to:

How to Have Your Tonsils Out
WITHOUT FREAKING OUT!!!

And she's right. That's what I had the most trouble with—the feelings part. It's harder to figure out feelings than it is to figure out facts.

"You could make it like a comic book! Like a story with pictures and everything!"

I could.

"And there could be activities to learn about the operation, and true information about the hospital. Almost like a magazine mixed with a comic book to—"

"To help other kids not worry so much," I say, finishing Quinny's sentence.

"Right! And we could have fun stuff in there, too, so we don't bore people to sleep. Like a word search! Oh, oh! We could also do a crossword puzzle and a coloring sheet. . . ."

Quinny keeps saying *we*. Then she stops and looks at me with big eyes.

"Hopper, what if we did this together? I have a million ideas."

I do, too. This could be interesting.

"You'll draw it, and I'll do the words," says Quinny. "Let's start by me interviewing you—tell me everything!"

"I'm not supposed to talk yet, remember?"

"Then let's start with the title. Every book needs a title."

She's right. I open my sketchbook and write:

HOW TO HAVE YOUR TONSILS OUT
WITHOUT FREAKING OUT
By Hopper Grey and Quinny Bumble

"Wait a second. Why does your name go first?" she asks.

"Because."

"It should be alphabetical order. And Bumble comes before Grey."

"But I'm the one who had my tonsils out."

We make a compromise. My name will go first, but Quinny's name will be BIGGER.

She also thinks we need some exclamation

119

points. I add one, just to quiet her down.

"Now, let's make a table of contents," she says. "Every book has one of those, too."

Actually, no, some books don't—but I think ours could use one.

Making a table of contents is harder than it sounds because it means we have to figure out all the stuff that's going to be inside the book.

We get to work on it. We work our brains out.

When I look up, it's dark out. My room is a mess.

Time flies when you're figuring out what to do with leftover tonsils.

Quinny's father shows up and says she has to leave. Mom is with him in the doorway and says I have to rest. She threatens to take away my charcoal pencils and all our paper.

"What are you kids doing in here, anyway?"

"No, don't look!" Quinny blocks our pages from Mom's eyes. "It's a top secret tonsils project. Believe me, Mrs. Grey, when we have news to share, you'll be the first to know."

Mom looks at Quinny suspiciously now.

"You have my word," Quinny adds.

"Drawing is okay, talking is not," Mom says to me. "You need to rest your throat."

But the more time I spend with Quinny, the better my throat feels. And the less rest I need. She's like magic that way, I think.

Eighteen

Quinny

On Sunday, Mrs. Porridge calls me after lunch, right when I'm about to go back to Hopper's house to work some more on our top secret tonsils project.

"I could use your help, Quinny. Guess who's coming back this afternoon?"

It takes me just one try to guess.

"Correct," she says. "I think the headache I've had all morning is about to get worse."

"Don't worry, Mrs. Porridge. Help is on the way. I'll be right over."

This time, Victoria shows up in her rubber rain boots. Plus plastic gloves and a doctor's face mask.

122

That girl is ready for those chickens.

Walter growls at her. I don't think he recognizes Victoria in her new outfit. Then Disco screeches at Walter, and they start having a debate, but not exactly like civilized human beings. Mrs. Porridge scoops Walter up and puts him in the house.

Then Cha-Cha jumps onto Victoria's shoulder as she's bent over cleaning the feeder.

"No! Off, chicken, off!"

Cha-Cha obeys and hops off Victoria's shoulder—and onto her head.

"*Nooooo!* Off!"

"Hey, Victoria, you forgot to bring a helmet." I laugh.

That chicken flaps her happy feathers, all excited, like a mountain climber who just reached the top. Victoria's head wiggles and shakes and shrieks some more.

"Get off me! OFFFFFFF!"

"Aww, Victoria, I think Cha-Cha likes you. The only other person she ever jumps onto is Walter, and she looooooves him."

"GET THAT CHICKEN OFF ME RIGHT NOW!"

That's when Cha-Cha does what chickens sometimes do, wherever they happen to be standing. Mrs. Porridge was right. There is no such thing as a magic invisible chicken toilet.

Nineteen

Hopper

This time, the screaming sounds like an opera singer falling off a cliff while holding a microphone.

I stop drawing and look out my window. But I can't see through all the trees.

A few minutes later, Quinny shows up at my door, breathless. She was supposed to come over right after lunch to work on our tonsils book.

"Where were you?" I ask.

"Don't be mad. Mrs. Porridge needed my help, and then—you'll never believe what happened— Cha-Cha pooped in Victoria's *hair*! Ha, that's what she gets for stealing my chickens. She's taking a shower right now in Mrs. Porridge's bathroom.

I've never even been in Mrs. Porridge's bathroom. Have you? By the way, what are you drawing?"

"I'm drawing what you see when you look up from the operating table."

"Good idea. But maybe make it less scary? So you don't scare people?"

It did feel a bit scary. I don't want to lie, or to forget, because I'm proud of myself for surviving it. "I still don't understand how they made me sleep and then woke me up."

"Hey, Hopper, I think your voice works better today! Can I interview you now?"

"Mom says I can't talk until next week."

"But you're talking right now. Plus, if we do it quietly, your mom won't even hear."

So I let Quinny interview me. I whisper about the hospital. About Dr. Merkle and Dr. Parva and Nurse Chuck. And the freezing-cold operating room filled with evil-looking machines that weren't really evil. And how sick I felt afterward from the anesthesia, but how my family was there. And how I'm starting to feel better now. A lot better.

I take a breath because that is a lot of talking I just did.

And then I think of something else to tell Quinny.

"The Brain Expo. Those tickets you got for my birthday—I bet the scientists there can explain it."

"Explain what?"

"How doctors make your brain fall asleep with anesthesia. And then wake you up. Why your brain obeys the anesthesia."

"Oh." Quinny has a funny look on her face now.

I start to write down questions.

How do you know everyone's brain works the same way?

What if some people's brains have a certain part missing or in a different place?

How can you tell how much falling-asleep medicine one person needs versus another person? Is there a formula? What if the medicine doesn't work on everyone?

I'll need a notebook for all the answers. Or maybe Mom will let me use her phone to record people saying the answers.

"Maybe you can help me talk to the scientists there?" I ask Quinny. "You're good at interviewing people."

Quinny doesn't say anything. Her eyes stare down at the ground.

"Maybe." She says it so softly I can barely hear.

"Thanks for getting those tickets. I can't wait for my birthday."

"Uh-huh."

"Quinny?"

"Hey, I just remembered I promised Piper I'd read her a pitcher book—I mean, a picture book. Gotta go."

And she races out of my room.

Something's wrong.

"Quinny, what's wrong?" I call out the window.

But she runs across the grass and into her own house without answering me.

Twenty

Quinny

Nothing's wrong. But I wish Hopper wouldn't talk so much about that Brain Expo. Because I told Victoria I'd go to her party, which is on the exact same Sunday afternoon in a few weeks, and I still haven't quite figured out how to be in two places at once.

Maybe I can give Caleb my ticket and he can go with Hopper. But then Hopper would be sad, since those tickets were a birthday gift from me. I saw that his mom even wrote it on their kitchen wall calendar in bright red marker: *Oct 24 h's bday—brain expo w quinny.*

I should've told Victoria I already have plans

during her party. But I love pets, costumes, and food—it's like that party was made just for me! The other thing is, I'm a little scared of seeing a brain that isn't in someone's head. But Hopper thinks the human body is fascinating, and I'll never forget the look on his face when I gave him those Brain Expo tickets. I made him happy. Not a lot of people can do that. It's practically a superpower.

Monday morning at school, lots of kids are absent. And lots of kids who are here are wearing braids or bandannas, or have slimy, slicked-back hair.

At morning meeting, Mrs. Meanie Sub tells us some new rules. No hugs. No sharing personal items, like barrettes or hats. And stay away from people, especially their heads.

People's heads = lunch for hungry lice.

But staying away from people is not one of my strengths.

"It's an epidemic," says Victoria on the way back to our desks.

"A what?"

"Get away from my head," she says. "And go read a dictionary."

In the hall on the way to gym, I notice a line of glum kids waiting by Nurse Mira's office. I see extra ladies in there with combs and magnifying glasses and frowny faces.

Wow. That's the biggest head-check line I've ever seen.

Principal Ramsey is also nearby, talking to some other grown-ups I don't even know.

"Principal Ramsey? Is it true? Are fleas taking over the whole school like teeny-tiny flesh-eating zombies?" I tug a tiny bit at his suit, just in case he didn't notice my voice.

He leans down to me with a serious look. "Just between you and me, Quinny, this is the worst lice outbreak I've seen in my two decades at Whisper Valley Elementary."

Just hearing those words makes me feel itchy.

During language arts, I get to tell Mrs. Flavio my new *how-to* topic. I show her the title and the whole table of contents that Hopper and I did together.

HOW TO HAVE YOUR TONSILS OUT
WITHOUT FREAKING OUT
By Hopper Grey and **QUINNY BUMBLE**

Table of contents
(Just a rough draft. We still need to
fix and fancy this up.)

1) Tonsils 101: Open Wide! Here, Hopper
   draws the inside of your mouth and throat.
   What's really in there, anyway? A whole lot
   of slime, to be honest.
2) How Well Do You Know Your Tonsils
   Trivia? Play a little game of True or False
   and find out.
3) Ask an Expert: Dr. Merkle has been an
   ENT doctor for eighteen years—that's a lot
   of tonsils!
4) What Really Happens at the Hospital?
   Here we show the inside of the operating

132

room and interview some extra experts, like Nurse Chuck and anesthesiologist Dr. Parva.

5) *Been There, Done That.* Here we interview a kid who survived a tonsillectomy—and you will, too! Then he draws what it was really like with his own awesome set of charcoal pencils.

6) *Ice-cream Word Search Time!* Here are two, because we couldn't decide which one to use.

7) *Hate Bunnies?* Enter our design-your-own-hospital-gown contest! Guest judge is fashion designer and president of ViP Fashions Victoria Porridge, but we still have to ask her.

8) *Last but not least: What to Do with Leftover Tonsils!* Imagine if you could actually keep your tonsils. Here are just some of the endless possibilities for what you could do with these special slimy souvenirs. (We put this in because laughter is the best medicine.)

I wait for Mrs. Flavio to read the whole thing and be impressed, but after only a few seconds, she looks at me. "Eleanor, what is the meaning of this?"

"The meaning is, it's a table of contents—"

"Don't get smart with me. Each student is required to do his or her own work."

"I did, and so did Hopper—"

"Hopper is absent—"

"Oh, he'll be back soon! He lives next door to me. That's how we did this together."

Mrs. Meanie Sub checks her big teacher book. "I see you're already late in turning in your topic. As you'll learn, I'm a firm believer in following directions and respecting rules."

"I had a topic on time! I really did! But I didn't want to hurt Piper's feelings, and then Victoria stole my chickens, and then, over the weekend, I was playing with Hopper and—"

"Enough!" Mrs. Meanie Sub booms.

The whole class looks over at us. My face feels swollen now.

"Eleanor—back to your seat. Please find a

coherent, suitable topic of your own by tomorrow, or you get a zero."

A zero? I don't even know what *coherent* means.

"Everybody else, line up. It's time to go outside."

Everybody lines up, all excited for recess.

But for my recess, Mrs. Flavio makes me stay inside and sit in a chair.

I slump at my desk. I press my hands on my ears so I don't hear all the excitement.

I am not going to cry. It's okay to cry in school if you need to, but I don't want to cry in front of Victoria. (Whenever I'm upset, she stares so hard I think her nosy eyes might explode.)

Maybe one or two tears leak out anyway.

"You can have the chickens back."

I rub my face and look up. Victoria is hovering over my desk. "I'm going to write 'How to Build a Fashion Empire' after all. It turns out chickens are not my kind of animal."

Grrrr. No kidding. I could have told her that *before* she stole those chickens.

"They're stubborn," says Victoria. "And way too poopy. They're all yours."

She puts a piece of candy on my desk. It's maple candy, my favorite.

For every two or three awful things Victoria does, she does one nice thing. Sometimes that girl is even more confusing than Hopper.

"Victoria, back in line, please," Mrs. Flavio calls out. "Time to go."

Then that meanie sub catches me chewing Victoria's candy and makes me spit it out. Of course she does. Because that's the kind of rotten-lucky day I'm having.

Twenty-one

Hopper

My room used to be my favorite place in the world. But now that I've been trapped in here, like Mom's priSONer, for the last few days, I miss school. Even the loud parts.

And I never want to see another Popsicle again as long as I live.

"Hopper, how are you feeling?"

It's Mom at my door again. With a Popsicle and this look on her face, like I'm not resting enough. But I don't feel sick anymore. My throat feels better, and I've been working on the tonsils book. I've got six panels of illustrations done and several more sketched in.

Still, when Mom walks in, I hide my sketch-book and lie there like she wants me to.

"Are you resting, sweetie? Would you like another Popsicle?"

No and no. I would like a rest from being forced to rest.

Mom tells me she has to drive the twins to soccer because their carpool family got lice. "But Mrs. Porridge will be right downstairs if you need anything. And I'll be back soon, and you can always call my cell if you—"

"Mom, relax. He'll be fine." Ty comes up behind her, wearing his soccer clothes.

"Yeah, Ma. Leave him alone," Trevor adds. Then he says to me, "Wanna use the Xbox?"

I shake my head. The last few days, Ty and Trevor have been acting so strange that I can't believe they're the same brothers who used to toss me around like a beanbag.

Who are these people, and what did they do with my real brothers?

"Try to get some rest, okay?" says Mom.

I let her hug me good-bye. Then I watch from the window as they drive away.

139

I also see Mrs. Porridge out in the yard, weeding our vegetable patch. She waves up at me and asks if I'm hungry—I shake my head no. She asks if I feel like playing cards—no. She says that in that case she'll be out there weeding my mother's sorry excuse for a vegetable patch because it pains her to look at such an unkempt garden.

This means that, right now, I have the whole house to myself.

I go out into the hall and into my parents' room. I dial a number on their phone.

"Dr. Merkle's office," says Trudy's voice on the phone. "How may I help you?"

"Can I please speak to Dr. Merkle? This is Hopper Grey. He took my tonsils out."

"Oh, hello there, Hopper. Dr. Merkle is with a patient. Can I help you with anything?"

"No thank you. I just need to talk to him."

"Is everything okay, sweetie?"

"Yes, but can you please tell him it's important?"

I hear a noise from downstairs. I don't want Mrs. Porridge to know what I'm doing, so I hurry off the phone and back to my room, but in the hallway I bump into Quinny.

"Hopper, what were you doing on the phone?"

Seeing Quinny startles me. I keep going to my room, but a second later she barges in and flops onto my beanbag chair, which I didn't give her permission to do.

"You're supposed to ring the doorbell before you walk into someone's house."

"Mrs. Porridge said I could come in. Now, brace yourself—I have some tragic news. Mrs. Meanie Sub kicked me off the tonsils book, so I can't do it with you anymore."

"What?"

"She's making us do our own separate *how-to* assignments—no sharing."

"But a lot of the ideas in there are yours."

"She doesn't care."

"If they kick you off, then I'm kicking myself off, too."

"You can't kick yourself off—they're *your* tonsils." Quinny slouches. "I should have known that meanie sub would never let me do this. She hates me. I bet if Victoria asked to do the book with a partner, she would say 'Yes, of course, Victoria, do anything you want.' Oh, Hopper, when are you coming back? I like school so much better when you're there!"

My stomach backflips to hear her say this. I like any place better when Quinny is there, too. But I don't actually tell her this. It's scary enough that I think it. My feelings feel breakable and private, and I'm not going to holler them out into the world.

Who knows what people would do with my feelings if they knew about them?

There are people in the world like Victoria, who will chew your feelings up and spit them out. There are people like Alex Delgado, who I'm talking to more at school, but still, he's only friendly sometimes and he calls people names like *moron* and *idiot*. I know he's got those ugly words inside him like a weapon, and who knows when he'll aim them at me?

There's another boy at school, Caleb, who moved here from California, and Quinny thinks he's nice. But Caleb plays soccer in the same league as my brothers, and he's becoming friends with Alex Delgado, too. That's not a great sign.

Quinny's really the only one I can trust. But I'm not going to tell *her* that.

142

"What if we still did the tonsils book together?" I say.

"Ha. I'd get a zero."

"Not for school or anything. Just to do it."

Quinny's eyes shine. "You mean, like, for fun?"

"And to help other kids. Did you know that eighty thousand people get their tonsils taken out every year, just in the United States? And most of those people are kids."

"Wow, Hopper, that's a lot of tonsils! So a comic book, a coloring book, AND a magazine book about tonsils all rolled into one. By kids, for kids. So you know it's honest."

"We could give it to Dr. Merkle."

"Ooh, and the school librarian!" yells Quinny.

"I was thinking about it today. I called Dr. Merkle to interview him for the book. I have an appointment with him on Friday, and we could show it to him then. Maybe he'll even put it in his waiting room."

"Hopper, you mean Dr. Merkle might publish your book?"

"*Our* book. And no, silly—he's an ear, nose, and throat doctor, not a book publisher."

"Why can't he be both?"

I think for a second. "I don't know."

"Or I could publish it!" Quinny declares. "There's a copy shop on the way to that college where my mom works—"

"Quinny, you're not a publisher, either. You're just a kid."

"So what? It only costs a dime to publish a page on the machine at the copy shop. I went there with Mom to copy Piper's birth certificate so she could start kindergarten early because she's an evil genius. By the way, how much money do you have?"

"Quinny—"

"And how many total pages do you think our book will be when it's done?"

"Quinny—"

"I think we should keep it short and funny. Nobody likes long books—"

"Hey, I like long books—"

"A short book with lots of jokes, and we can sneak in the serious information—"

"Quinny, can I talk, too? Or are you going to keep having a conversation by yourself?"

"Of course you can talk! It's not my fault you never jump in."

"Okay, let's do this," I jump in. "Let's figure it out."

"YAYYYYYYY! But Hopper, if we want that tonsils book ready to show Dr. Merkle by Friday, we've got to act fast! We don't have time to wait for the Brain Expo. We should go back to the hospital to interview Nurse Chuck and Dr. Parva and find those tonsils right away. I'm free this afternoon!"

"Very funny."

"It's not too far. The hospital is just a few blocks past school. Imagine if we had a picture of you holding a jar with your real-life tonsils. That book would be a best-seller."

"My parents won't let me go anywhere until my throat is totally healed."

Quinny looks out the window. "Well, they aren't home right now, are they?"

I look out at Mrs. Porridge in the garden, too. "There's no way she'll take us there."

"I know," says Quinny. "But *he* might."

"He?"

"Listen." She puts a hand to her ear and gestures out to something in the distance.

I listen. But all I hear is the faraway sound of someone hammering.

Twenty-two

Quinny

I lead Hopper out to Mrs. Porridge in the garden, all careful and polite. "Oh, hello again, Mrs. Porridge. It's so lovely to see you. How are you doing today?"

There is a smudge of dirt on her face as she looks up from under her sun hat, which is almost the size of a beach umbrella. "What are you up to now, Quinny?"

"Absolutely nothing! We're just going to say hi to the chickens if it's okay with you."

"Hopper, you feeling okay?" Mrs. Porridge looks at him kind of closely.

"He feels great," I answer for him. "But he could use some fresh air. Right, Hopper?"

Hopper looks a little queasy, which I think proves my point.

"*Hmmp*, well, okay," says Mrs. Porridge. "But don't stay too long. Ten minutes. That stubborn old coot is still over there hammering away, trying to build the Taj Mahal."

"Thanks, Mrs. Porridge!"

I take Hopper's hand and pull him away. All we have to do is go tell the stubborn old coot—I mean, Grandpa Gooley—about our tonsils book and how we need to interview Nurse Chuck and Dr. Parva (and find those leftover tonsils!), and that Hopper is feeling A-okay to take a little drive over to the hospital quick-quick before his parents even notice.

But just as we get to Mrs. Porridge's yard, Grandpa Gooley drives off in his truck.

"Grandpa Gooley!" I chase after him. "Grandpa Gooley, stop!"

Twenty-three

Hopper

Without Grandpa Gooley, there's no way for us to get to the hospital.

"Wait a sec. . . . My daddy's bike is in the garage," says Quinny. "And it has a sidecar for Piper, and I'm great at pedaling, and we'll be back before anyone finds out, I promise."

"Are you nuts? That's dangerous, and we'll get in trouble."

I argue with Quinny. She argues back. She pulls me over to her garage and shows me her dad's bike. But that bike is way too big for Quinny. The sidecar is too tiny for me.

No way am I agreeing to this. Never in a million years.

* * *

A few minutes later, I'm curled into a ball and bumping along in the tiny, windy sidecar as Quinny pedals her dad's giant bike down the street. Cars whizz by us.

Quinny has a way of getting people to do crazy stuff, I guess.

I picture the look on Mrs. Porridge's face when she finds the note Quinny left for her on the chicken porch, saying we'll be right back from the hospital.

I picture the look on Dad's face when Mrs. Porridge tells on us.

I feel a little sick to my stomach, and it's not from the bumpy ride.

We get to the hospital, and Quinny turns to me. "Okay, now what? Do you remember where the throat department is?"

"There's no such thing as the throat department."

"We'll look for Nurse Chuck, then. I bet he knows where they keep the body parts!"

Quinny hides the bike in some bushes and drags me inside the lobby of the hospital.

She smiles at the man behind the front desk.

"Hello and good afternoon, sir! We're here to see Nurse Chuck and Dr. Parva in the throat department, because Hopper just had his tonsils out and now we're writing a tonsils book that's going to help millions of kids everywhere. Can you please give us directions?"

The man looks confused. "Where are your parents?"

"Oh, my mom is just . . . parking the car. Yes, that's it."

"Have a seat until she arrives." The man points.

"Okay, great, thanks . . . but we really have to use the bathroom. It's an emergency."

The man points again.

"Thanks," says Quinny. "We'll be back in two seconds, super quick."

By the bathroom doors, there is a big rolling bin and Quinny yanks me to duck behind it, so no one can see us. "Hopper, I just had an idea for where those tonsils-in-a-jar could be. I bet they're down in the basement! They always keep creepy stuff like body parts in basements. Look, there's an exit sign for the stairs. Let's just go down there and look—"

"We're not allowed to go into the basement."

But Quinny drags me through that exit door. And down the stairs.

The door at the very bottom is locked and reads NO ADMITTANCE—HOSPITAL STAFF ONLY.

"Phooey," says Quinny. "I guess there's nowhere to go but up. Do you remember what floor you were on for your operation? Let's try that floor next."

"Quinny, no, we have to get back home before Mrs. Porridge gets worried."

I pull her back up the stairs. She argues the whole time, but I keep going.

I push through the door to the first floor. But then I realize something's wrong. Everything looks different. This isn't the right hall, or the same floor we were on.

"Quinny? Where are we?"

"The hospital, silly."

"But this doesn't look like the first floor. Or were we on the ground floor?"

I lead Quinny down the hall and turn the corner. This still doesn't look right. We need to get back to the stairs. I look around some more.

We're lost. We're by ourselves, breaking all the rules. My heart is pounding.

I see a tall security guard standing by some elevators, but she doesn't notice us.

"Oh, oh, Hopper, look! Look right over there!"

I turn to look, hoping that maybe Quinny found Dr. Parva or Nurse Chuck.

"It's a vending machine!" she cries. "I love those—do you have any coins? And look, there's a whole entire cafeteria here, too."

"We need to go home. This was a stupid idea."

"Let's take a quick break to have a snack. Then we'll keep looking."

She pulls me into the cafeteria and toward a tall stack of brown trays.

"Wait, Quinny, we don't have any money."

"Let's just pick out a few things, and then we'll go see if Nurse Chuck can loan us some."

Quinny stretches up on her toes and reaches for a tray from a tall stack, but she bumps another stack of trays next to it, and they all come crashing down to the floor.

People around us stop what they're doing and stare.

"Oops." Quinny giggles.

"Can I help you?" The tall security guard is looking down at us now.

Twenty-four

Quinny

I look up at that big, serious security guard. She doesn't look too friendly.

"No thank you. We're fine." I point to Hopper. "He just had an operation."

Hopper nods, but I don't know why that boy looks so nervous.

"Quinny?"

It's someone else's voice now. . . . Believe it or not, it's Ms. Yoon's!

There she is, by the vending machine, holding a bag of bright orange Cheesy-O's! She looks shocked to see me, too. I run over and hug that precious teacher. "Ms. Yoon! It's you, it's really you! But why are you holding a bag of Cheesy-O's? Mom never lets me eat those."

Ms. Yoon moves the bag of Cheesy-O's behind her back super quick.

"Quinny, Hopper, what on earth are you two doing here?"

"We're just here to get Hopper's tonsils back, which he forgot at the hospital last week. By the way, why did you leave school so fast like that—ohhhhhhh . . ."

That's when I realize Ms. Yoon's big, round beach ball tummy now looks like a deflated beach ball, and all of a sudden I know why she left school last week.

"Ms. Yoon! Where is that baby? Can we see it? Did you leave it in your hospital room? Congratulations! Is it a boy or a girl? Can we go to your room? We're free right now!"

"Quinny, the baby is upstairs in the nursery, and he's fine—"

"It's a he! I love baby boys! Good job, Ms. Yoon! Let's go see him right now."

"Where are your parents? Hopper—how was

your tonsillectomy? Shouldn't you be at home resting? What are you kids doing here by yourselves?"

Those are all good questions, but I don't think Ms. Yoon is going to like the answers.

"Quinny! Hopper! There you are!"

It's a cranky voice booming now. Mrs. Porridge is speeding toward us. Steam is practically shooting out of her ears. I'm guessing she saw the note I left for her on the chicken porch. Maybe if I stay calm, she'll stay calm.

"Hello, Mrs. Porridge, how are you? This is our teacher from school, Ms. Yoon."

"I was about to call the police!" she snaps, then offers her hand to Ms. Yoon. "Myrna Porridge, how do you do? These children claimed to be going to see the chickens, but—"

"But then we remembered this very important thing we had to do at the hospital, and since Daddy's bike was just sitting there in the garage—"

"You *biked* over here? By yourselves?"

"No, not by ourselves, there were lots of cars on the road, too."

Mrs. Porridge makes a little noise like she can't get enough air.

"And then we ran into Ms. Yoon! And we didn't want to be rude, so we stopped and chatted! Did you know she has a fabulous brand-new baby upstairs in this very hospital? And she just invited us up to come see him, didn't you, Ms. Yoon?" I clasp my hands together and look up at her, all hopeful.

And Ms. Yoon gets a confused look on her face. "Well, he is just upstairs. . . ."

"We couldn't possibly impose," says Mrs. Porridge. "My apologies, please excuse us."

"Wait . . . why not? You're here. You're all welcome to come see him—"

"Oh, thank you, Ms. Yoon! Come on. Let's go right now before you change your mind."

Mrs. Porridge grumps and frets and snaps, but I pull her along, too.

Ms. Yoon takes us in the elevator to the nursery, and we look through a window at all the babies lined up in rows in clear plastic containers, which look kind of like those containers that Mom stores stuff in down in our basement. Only these containers don't have blue rubber lids like ours do—they're open on top, so the babies can breathe, I guess.

There are rows and rows of brand-new baby-doll faces . . . each of them squishy, round, and reddish . . . reddish vanilla or reddish caramel or reddish chocolate. Some are quiet, some are howling, some wiggle, some just lay there staring up at life.

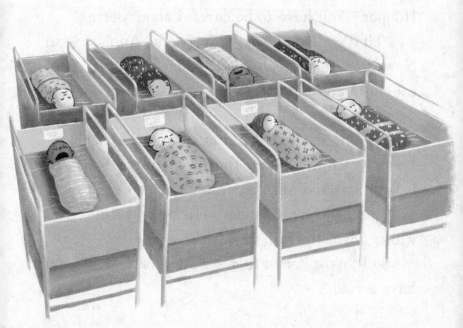

I can't believe each tiny blob is going to be a whole entire person one day.

"Ms. Yoon, they're all so cute! Which one is yours?"

Ms. Yoon points to him in the middle. He's super blobby and the color of a peach.

"Oh, he's definitely the cutest one! Can I hold him?"

"Not today, Quinny."

"When my friend Owen got a baby brother, I wasn't allowed to hold him right away," says Hopper. "You have to be careful about germs."

"That's silly," I say. "My friend Anu back in New York had a baby sister who was born right in her apartment, and we got to hold her the same day."

We stand there looking at all the babies— I really think they're the best things I've ever looked at—and after a while, Mrs. Porridge puts her hand on my shoulder. Then she sniffles and walks down the hall to a bathroom.

So I follow her in there. "Mrs. Porridge, do you have a cold?"

She's blowing her nose into some toilet paper and won't look at me.

"Mrs. Porridge, are you okay?" I wait for her to answer. "Oh, your eyes—maybe you're allergic to babies?"

Mrs. Porridge splashes her face at the sink and then dries it off. "What if something had happened to you kids?" Her voice sounds all cracked. "What if you'd been hit by a car or . . ."

"But we're fine. Nothing happened. I'm so sorry for worrying you."

I can't stand how upset she looks, so I barge in and hug her, which is the first time I have ever touched that big old grown-up lady. "I'm very, very, extra-very sorry. I didn't mean to scare you, honest." She feels so comfy and so sad, and we stay in that hug. She puts her hand on my head, all gentle.

"This doesn't mean you're off the hook," she says. "You're still in big trouble."

"I know."

"Where's the bike?"

"Outside, in the bushes."

Mrs. Porridge sighs.

Twenty-five
Hopper

I stand next to Ms. Yoon, watching all the babies through the window.

"They won't remember any of this, will they?"

"Nope."

"Why do we start remembering when we get older?"

Ms. Yoon looks at me. "Well, Hopper, it has to do with how our brains develop."

I know that. But there's so much more to know. I wonder if I'll ever feel like I understand how it all works: people, the world, everything.

I wish I could remember all the way back to being a baby.

What did I know back then, before I could remember what I knew?

I guess I'll never know.

Quinny and Mrs. Porridge come back from the bathroom.

"Ms. Yoon! Oh good, you're still here!" says Quinny. "I forgot to ask you something super important. When are you coming back to school? Because that sub they gave us is a giant meanie, and we really miss you."

"Guys, I miss you, too. But please try to get along with the sub, for now."

"Why don't you just bring the baby to school, like you did when he was still a beach ball? We could set up a crib in the classroom—"

"Quinny—"

"I could help—I have two little sisters, you know. I can even change diapers! Come on, Ms. Yoon. It'd be even better than having a guinea pig in the room."

"Quinny, that's enough," says Mrs. Porridge. "It's time to leave Ms. Yoon in peace."

* * *

On the way home, Mrs. Porridge is not in a good mood. She says we lied and tricked her, and put ourselves in danger by running off without permission. She says she expects more from us than that kind of unacceptable nonsense.

"Furthermore, the hospital does not have Hopper's tonsils," she says. "What a ridiculous idea. Wait till I tell your parents how you ran off like that."

"No, please don't—it was just one tiny little mistake!" Quinny cries.

"A *big* mistake," huffs Mrs. Porridge.

"But if you tattle on us, then we'll be punished and grounded, and we won't be able to come and take care of the chickens, and those poor chickens will get lonely and hungry and smelly, and your screened-in porch will smell like a GIANT pile of poop, and you don't want that, do you? Please, Mrs. Porridge, think of those poor, innocent chickens!"

Quinny elbows me and makes a face. "Think of the chickens," I say.

Mrs. Porridge gives Quinny a sharp look in the mirror. She pretends to scoff, but I can tell it is really more of a laugh.

Luckily, we beat my parents home, so nobody has to find out about this trip at all. Mom would freak out if she knew Mrs. Porridge let her priSONer escape.

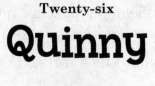

Twenty-six
Quinny

"Screeee-creeee-creeeee-screee!"

Disco wakes me up way too early again on Tuesday. So I have a little talk with her while doing my chicken chores.

"Disco, do you really want Mrs. Porridge to send you away?"

"Scree-SCREEEE," screeches Disco with an attitude.

"Shhh! You better cut this out before she turns you into chicken pot pie."

"SCREEEEEEEEEEEE!" Disco turns and shrieks extra huge at the porch window that looks into Mrs. Porridge's house.

166

"*Sssssssssss,*" hisses Walter, whose furry face fills up the other side of that window.

"Calm your engines down, both of you! You're better than this!"

I check the nest box in the mini-henhouse for eggs—nope. I set out fresh feed. Cha-Cha comes over and bumps into my legs, which is her way of hugging.

"Good morning, beautiful. When are you going to grow up and make me an egg?"

"*Brrr bip,*" replies Cha-Cha.

Hopper shows up and I hand him the watering dish. "Fill 'er up. And guess what, I think Disco and Walter are now officially enemies."

"Roosters don't have a lot of friends," says Hopper.

"Disco could just be a very loud, very bossy hen," I say. "With a very large comb."

"Wake up, Quinny, and smell the coffee," says Mrs. Porridge, walking onto the porch with a cup of hers.

"I only like hot chocolate," I point out.

"A rooster is a rooster is a rooster," she says.

"An egg is an egg is an egg," I say to Cha-Cha. "But no rush."

After the chicken chores, it's time for school, but Hopper still has to stay home. He invites me over that afternoon to work some more on the tonsils book.

"Absolutely," I say. "You can work on the drawings while I'm in school. And then we can work on the words and ideas together later, deal?"

"Deal," he says. "Bye."

"Hopper, wait—can you come hang out with me at the bus stop, at least?"

"I doubt it. Mom barely lets me out for the chickens."

Phooey. I wish I could stay home with him.

But after I get on the school bus, I look out as we pass Hopper's house. I look for him in all the windows of his house that face the street—and he is right there in one of them, in his living room window! And he waves, like he was looking for me, too. It makes me feel like we're still together, even though we're really not.

It makes me think today is going to be a good day.

In school, I can't help it—I tell people all about how I got invited to see Ms. Yoon's brand-new baby and how Hopper and I are working together on an amazing book that his doctor is going to publish. Victoria's eyes are stuck right on me as I talk.

I talk and talk and talk. I feel very special that my life is so exciting.

Then Victoria starts talking about the pet she's getting from the animal shelter and how she hasn't made up her mind yet if she wants a puppy, a kitten, or an Angora rabbit.

"Or maybe I'll just get one of each. My daddy said I can have whatever I want, and my house has plenty of space. I could probably start a whole petting zoo if I wanted."

Now my eyes are on her, hard. I bet she can feel my stare. My daddy hasn't even taken me to that animal shelter once yet.

The day gets worse when Mrs. Flavio keeps me inside for recess again. She gives me my *Minute*

Math sheet from yesterday (which I didn't finish in a minute) and says, "This is a perfect opportunity to improve our arithmetic. Let's make the most of it."

And I'm so glum that I slump there at my desk, for the second day in a row.

After I get home from school, I go straight into Daddy's office (which is really just a closet in the upstairs hallway), and I sit and wait forever for him to get off the phone.

"Daddy, can you take me to the animal shelter? I'm free right now!"

"Quinny, please."

"Please what? You promised last week."

"I'm in the middle of something important."

"But what if Victoria gets the very last puppy—"

"I have a big deadline. I can't just drop everything because you're whining."

"I don't want you to drop things. I just want to see the shelter, like you promised."

Daddy's hair is messy and his eyes are extra

170

saggy, and there's something about the tired, angry way they look at me that makes a lump bump up in my throat.

"Keep it up, Quinny. Just keep it up." It's like a warning, the way he says it.

A snack makes everything better. At least while I'm chewing it.

Then I go see what Hopper is doing, since I just remembered we're supposed to be working on the tonsils book this afternoon.

And it turns out he is on the phone, talking to Dr. Merkle about tonsillectomies. I wait for them to finish, and then Hopper tells me that Dr. Merkle is excited to see the tonsils book at his checkup on Friday. Which means we need to get to work right away so there is actually a tonsils book for that doctor to see!

Hopper and I work the whole afternoon.

Even though his mom tries to distract us.

Even though his brothers try to annoy us.

We ignore them all, and we work, work, work.

We think and we draw and we write. We think

171

some more and argue. We erase and cross things out and tear stuff up. We change our minds and change them back. We laugh.

Daddy isn't the only one with a big deadline.

Twenty-seven

Hopper

The way to make two hours feel like five minutes is to work on a project with Quinny. We don't agree on everything—she thinks the panels I'm drawing about the tonsillectomy are too scary; I think her tonsils True or False is too silly—but somehow she never hurts my feelings. Somehow we get a lot done.

I sleep really well that night and wake up Wednesday morning full of energy.

I'm feeling so much better it's like that operation never even happened. I ask Mom if I can go to school today. She makes a shocked smile and says, "Sorry, not yet." But at least she lets me out to help with the chicken chores again.

I meet Quinny at the porch coop. Disco and Walter are still at each other's throats and have to be separated. Cha-Cha is still pooping in her feed bowl. No eggs. We clean and refill the feeder, pour fresh water, and let the chickens outside for a bit. They scratch around while Quinny and I come up with a schedule.

First, we'll finish making the tonsils book today after she gets home from school. Then, tomorrow afternoon, we'll edit it, read it over for mistakes, and fix everything.

Then, on Friday, we'll show it to Dr. Merkle at my appointment, which Mom switched to three forty-five so Quinny can come, too.

"Sounds like a plan," says Quinny. "I can't wait!"

Then we hear Quinny's dad yelling that it's time to leave for school. Her face turns sour.

"Well, good-bye," she says. "Now I have to go spend my life with a sub who hates me."

"The sub doesn't hate you." I don't understand how anyone could hate Quinny.

"She hates my whole personality. She hates everything I do and say and think."

"Quinny, she's not a mind reader—she can't hate what you *think*."

"She stole my recess for two whole days."

"What? Why?"

"Because I chatted just a tiny bit. She said she'll take it away again if I talk. She looks at me like I'm a pest every time I raise my hand, so I just stopped raising it. I'm not going to talk at all anymore. Maybe then she'll like me."

I don't know what to say. That doesn't sound right.

"Did you tell anyone this?"

"Daddy would be mad if he knew I got in trouble. And Principal

Ramsey said I have to get along with the sub. Ms. Yoon did, too."

Quinny waves a small limp wave as she walks away.

"Bye." I wave back.

I think about her sad, droopy face as I walk home.

In the kitchen, I ask Mom, "Can I borrow your phone?"

"My phone? Hopper, what's going on?"

"Nothing. Just an idea."

Mom looks at me, a little too interested. "What's this idea about?"

But if I tell her, she might stop me from trying to do the idea. She might say things like, *It's none of your business; it's not appropriate; it's a waste of time.*

Then I realize I don't need Mom's phone. Because I know how to use the computer.

"Hopper?" She looks at me, waiting for an answer.

"Nothing. Never mind. I'm going to rest in my room."

I do go up to my room, but I don't rest. I think. I plan.

And I listen carefully for where Mom is in the house.

Her computer password is *PASSWORD*. I type it into the keyboard later that morning while she's down in the basement doing laundry.

Twenty-eight

Quinny

The school bus pulls up to our stop, and Daddy says something shocking.

"Remember you're going home with Victoria today."

"What?"

"For the playdate. And then Mom or I will pick you up before dinner."

"But you never even told me that—I made plans with Hopper for after school."

The bus door opens and the driver smiles good morning out at us.

"I told you earlier this week," says Daddy. "She invited you over to her house."

"No, you *didn't*. Because if you told me, I would have said *no way!*"

"Quinny, stop it. I've been pretty busy lately, in case you haven't noticed. Now, it's rude to cancel this late unless you're sick—you're going on that playdate."

Daddy's been *too* busy lately. And way too cranky. His main job is taking care of us at home while Mommy goes to her main job over at a college in the town next to Whisper Valley (which is called a name I can't remember right now). But all of a sudden Daddy has decided to get a second job, which is called *starting his own business*, and that is definitely interfering with his main job. For example, today he let Cleo suck on her Binky all morning, even though Mom wants her to stop using it during the day. And he packed me moldy grapes in my lunch box (luckily I replaced them with an extra serving of cookies). And then he had no idea that Piper wasn't wearing any clothes until I pointed it out.

"Quinny, *go*," Daddy says. "Victoria's sitter will pick you up from school."

"What about Hopper?"

"You'll play with him some other time. Have-a-good-day-I-love-you-now-*go*."

The bus is waiting for me to get on it. Even Piper is already on the bus, and people are kind of looking at me now, waiting.

Grrrrr. I stomp onto that bus. The thing that stinks about being a kid is you can make plans, but you usually need a grown-up to make those plans happen. Which is very, very, extra-very unfair.

I spend the whole day at school knowing I have to go home with Victoria.

It's not the happiest thing I've ever known, let me tell you.

But then a miracle happens to almost cheer me up. Mrs. Flavio pulls me aside and says no more recess detention, so I can join my class on the playground from now on. I'm so happy I almost try to hug that meanie sub, but she puts her hands out to stop me. "Calm down, Eleanor. Control yourself."

Then she tells me something else that is even better news than the recess miracle.

"I've been giving it some thought, and . . . since you and Hopper have already done a lot of work on the *how-to* project, I will make an exception."

"You mean, we can do our tonsils book together and you won't give me a zero?"

"That's right."

Two miracles in a row! There's no way Mrs. Flavio is getting away without a hug now. I throw my arms around that meanie sub, even though her horrified voice is huffing and puffing for me to stop.

* * *

181

However, during recess I end up wishing I wasn't even *at* recess.

Because Victoria is talking about her animal shelter fund-raising party again.

"McKayla, you're good at decorations. You'll work on those," says Victoria. "Kaitlin, you're good at drawing. You'll help with the invitation flyers. And, Quinny, you're good at . . ."

Victoria pauses. A really long time.

"Eating. You're good at eating food, I guess, so you can help design the menu."

"There's a menu for the party?" I ask.

"Not like a restaurant menu. It's just a list of all the food that we'll serve."

"How about cheese and crackers? Oh, and chicken wings—"

"Ugh. Quinny, sometimes I wonder if you really moved here from New York."

"Of course I did." I have no idea why that girl would wonder something so silly.

At the end of the day, all the big yellow buses rumble over to the front of the school and wait for us kids. But Victoria is not a busser. She gets picked up in a shiny black car by a lady in big black sunglasses, who tilts her head at me instead of saying hello. The lady tells me her name is Masha, and she gives us snacks to eat in the backseat. Two bento boxes full of avocado and cucumber slices on sunflower-seed crackers, which is a really strange but delicious and fancy snack no one has ever given me. (I think Disco and Cha-Cha would love these crackers, so I save a couple in my pocket.)

"Wow, Masha's such a great sitter," I say to Victoria, my mouth full of avocado and crackers. "I'm lucky if I get stale pretzels after school."

"Masha's not my sitter."

"Oh, okay. You mean, she's a relative . . . ?"

"She lives with us since my father travels so much for his job. She's just . . . my Masha."

Victoria's Masha drives us to Victoria's house.

I've never been to it before, but I've seen it. Everyone has.

Most of the town of Whisper Valley is actually in a valley, but a small part of town is on a big hill above that valley. And Victoria lives in the biggest house on that big hill.

My mouth hangs open as we pull into the driveway, because up close this place looks even more like a fancy wedding cake, with the swirliest frosting I've ever seen.

Victoria's wedding cake house > my barn house
Victoria's wedding cake house > Hopper's gingerbread house
Victoria's wedding cake house > the White House (probably)

"Oh, look, they're here!" Victoria bursts out of the car and runs onto her front porch, which is roomier than my whole living room (and has more furniture, too). She tears open a big envelope. "My new business cards! I designed them myself. Aren't they stunning?"

She shows them to me. They look like her old business cards, only fancier.

"But, Victoria, didn't you already have a bunch of business cards?"

"I gave myself a promotion."

Victoria used to be *president* of her company,

ViP Fashions. Now she's *CEO*. "Because a CEO is a much higher-level job than a president," she explains.

Even though Victoria is bragging, I have to admit her cards are kind of cool. They change color when you move them. They're textured and shiny and bright.

Also in Victoria's mail is a catalog for Halloween costumes and decorations.

"Let's go inside. We can flip through this while we have our snack," she says.

"I thought we had our snack in the car—but okay, sure!"

"That was just the appetizer. Now, Quinny, pay attention. I've organized the playdate into three parts. First, snack, because I know how much you love food. Second, a tour of my house, because it's amazing. Last but not least, we'll have another party-planning meeting, because we still have lots of work to do."

I feel like asking Victoria why there is no time to *play* on her playdate, but then her Masha brings out a big platter of fruit and cookies, and I forget to ask. We sit in the kitchen and flip through the Halloween catalog while we eat. Victoria marks the things she wants in it with a black marker. And, wow, she marks more things she wants for Halloween than I've ever even put on my Christmas list.

"What are you going to be for Halloween?" she asks me.

"Oh, I don't know yet."

That's not true—probably a chicken, but I don't want to give Victoria any ideas.

"Since my animal shelter party is right before Halloween, I've decided it's going to be a costume party for the animals *and* people," she says. "You can dress to match your pet, or for those sad people who don't have any pets, just wear any old Halloween costume."

Boy, I wish I had a pet to bring to Victoria's party. (Maybe Mrs. Porridge will lend me Cha-Cha?) Also, I wish I could be in two places at once, so Quinny #1 could go to her party while Quinny #2 goes with Hopper to the Brain Expo. For a second, I'm actually kind of jealous of those bully twins who live next door to me.

After we finish our snack, Victoria gives me a
tour of her house. And it's a loooong one. The list
of things I learn on her tour is very, very, extra-
very fascinating, plus a bit sad:

1) Victoria's great-great-grandfather built
   this house and started the town of
   Whisper Valley in 1872. There's an old
   picture of him with a twirly mustache
   by the living room fireplace. "He was
   a mountain climber, a champion poker
   player, and a genius at business," she says.
   "He's my role model."
2) Victoria is actually named after her house,
   which is her mother's favorite style of
   house: a Victorian.
3) I should say, it *was* her mother's favorite
   style of house, because Victoria's mother
   is dead. She died when Victoria was little,
   but there are pictures of her everywhere,
   and I can tell she was even more elegant
   than Victoria is.
4) Victoria also has a dead cat. It was her
   mother's cat, which was white and fluffy

and which didn't die until last year, and
its name was—

At this point in the tour, I get really sad.

"Quinny, get that mopey look off your face."

I swallow my sniffle. I didn't know Victoria
has a dead mother and a dead cat.

"Stop it." She moves her face closer to mine.
"Don't you dare feel sorry for me."

"I don't."

"Put those tears *away*."

Victoria says that her charming, wise, brilliant, generous mother always kept her chin up
and never felt sorry for herself, because it was a
waste of time, and a person should never waste
time on things that are a waste of time.

"Victoria, what a coincidence—Mrs. Porridge
says the same thing sometimes. She must be
related to your mother?"

"She's my father's aunt. That's why we have
the same last name. Now, pull yourself together,
Quinny, and come check out the house organ."

The house what?

"You're going to love this." Victoria opens a set of big, wide doors that disappear.

"Whoa, wait—where did those doors go?" I ask.

"They're pocket doors," she says. "The walls are hollow, so they slide right inside."

"Neat!"

And then she shows me a piano. Which is actually an organ. Which is actually part of the house. It was built with musical pipes that go all the way through the walls, so when you press the organ's keyboard, it sounds like the whole house is singing.

I play the first few notes of "Imagine" by John Lennon on that organ. It sounds powerful and everywhere. And the best part is, it sounds kind of like my accordion at home.

"Victoria, I had no idea you lived inside a big, giant accordion."

"I told you my house was amazing."

After that, she shows me the kitchen dumb-waiter (it's like an elevator for food), and a secret tiny closet inside the coat closet, and a fireplace big enough to fit both of us inside it. She shows me her basement, which has sparkly lights, a Ping-Pong table, a pinball machine, an old-fashioned popcorn popper, and a whole second kitchen.

And all that's just the downstairs.

Upstairs, Victoria shows me her bedroom, which has a bed with its own lacy roof.

And her playroom, which has lots of dolls I'm not allowed to touch.

And her office/workshop—where she runs her company, ViP Fashions, and makes her fabulous fashion creations on not just one but TWO sewing machines.

All I can think of is that tiny room I share with Cleo. And the tiny kitchen my family eats in, and Daddy's office-in-a-closet that blocks the hallway so we have to step over him.

"You're so lucky," I tell her. "I had to switch rooms, and now I share a little room with icky-sticky-screamy Cleo because Piper can't even—"

But I stop myself before I blab our private family business to Victoria.

"Because Piper can't even what?" she asks.

"Nothing. Never mind." I change the subject. "What's behind those doors?"

190

Victoria shows me—and it's her own personal bathroom, which has the prettiest bathtub I've ever seen. It looks kind of like a dressy lady's shoe. I don't tell her that all five of us in my family share one bathroom, which is smaller than hers. I can't believe there are more bathrooms living in Victoria's house than there are people.

Eventually, we run out of things for Victoria to show me. She leads us back down to the kitchen and pulls out a notebook.

"Now, about the party menu . . . Quinny, what are your ideas?"

"Well, we should have lots of food, for sure. Like cheese and crackers. And pizza!"

"Pizza? Everyone always has pizza. And I'm allergic to dairy, don't forget. Let's do something more special. What kind of food do they have in New York City restaurants?"

I actually didn't go out to restaurants very much when I lived back in New York. The food we ate there is pretty much like the food we eat here: grocery-store food that my parents cook. But Victoria is waiting for a more interesting answer. I try to think of one. . . .

There's dim sum in Chinatown. We only do that once a year.

Italian tacos from that food truck by the subway museum. They sure smelled good, but Daddy packed me lunch for that field trip, so I didn't get to try any.

There's that Korean barbecue restaurant I went to once with Mom when it was Take Your Kids to Work Day. Everything I tasted there was super savory and salty.

There's that wacky restaurant downtown that has a million colorful Christmas lights up year-round. I forget the name of it, but I went there for a birthday party once.

But my favorite NYC food place is the guy with the hot dog cart by the Central Park Zoo.

"Ooh, that's a fun idea—we should get him to come to the party," says Victoria.

"Really?" I feel shocked whenever I impress Victoria—it almost never happens.

"Sure. It would be unique. What's his name? I'll have Masha take care of it."

Wow. I wish I had a Masha. She's like a parent, but without all the yelling and *no*'s.

"You'd better stay for dinner," says Victoria. "We still have lots of work to do."

"Oh, Victoria, I'd love to, but I can't. I have to go see—" I stop my mouth from talking.

Victoria stares at me hard. "Hopper?" she guesses.

"Sorry. It's just, we're on a deadline—the tonsils book we're writing is due Friday."

"Mrs. Flavio said our projects aren't due until next week," says Victoria.

"Oh right—well, I meant the book publisher wants it by Friday. Yeah, that's it."

"What's the name of your publisher?"

I freeze for a moment. "ENT Books Corporation," I finally reply.

Victoria looks at me some more. "I've never heard of that publisher."

"Well, they publish mostly doctor-type books."

I don't know why I'm making things up to Victoria. Once I start, it's hard to stop. The more I lie, the worse I feel. Finally, I change the subject to something that isn't a lie.

"Hey, Victoria! I was wondering, can you be the guest judge for our hospital-gown-design contest?

That's one of the things we're doing in the book, where kids can design hospital gowns and send in a drawing, and we decide which designs are the best."

Victoria looks at me like I'm not making any sense.

"Because, you know, sometimes hospitals only have one kind of kids' gowns, and not everyone likes to wear bunnies? And you know about clothes a whole lot, so I thought . . ."

"Well, that is true." She smiles a little, but then her face gets serious again. "I'll have to check my schedule. What's the salary for this job?"

I have no idea what *salary* means.

"And is your book more like a magazine or is it a real book?" she asks again.

"Kind of in between. Like a combination magazine, book, and comic book."

"Well, if it's a magazine, you should put advertising in it, to make some money."

"Oh, we're not doing it to make money. We're just trying to help cheer up kids—"

"How about ads for ice-cream brands, since kids eat lots of ice cream after getting their tonsils out? Or hospitals could advertise, since there are lots of them to choose from."

I never thought of that. Don't people just usually pick the closest hospital?

"You could even advertise eggs for sale from your poopy, stubborn chickens."

"They haven't laid any eggs yet. We're just going to give the eggs away anyway."

Victoria snorts. "Quinny, grow up. No one gives away stuff they could actually sell."

"But people gave us lots of stuff back in the city," I say. "Like we got a Pack 'n Play® from our neighbors upstairs. My parents used to give stuff away all the time, too."

"Well, that explains why they don't have any money for a bigger house, and you have to share a room with that icky-sticky-screamy baby sister."

Victoria's sentence feels like a kick in my chest. It hurts so much I can't even talk.

But she acts like nothing bad happened and just keeps on having a conversation.

"Quinny, are you listening? I asked for the name of the hot dog cart owner."

"I have to go to the bathroom." I run out of the kitchen.

Then I run right back into the kitchen and ask, "Where's the closest bathroom?"

"Just around the corner. Third door on the left."

In the bathroom, I try to catch my breath. I do call my sister *icky-sticky-screamy Cleo* sometimes, but that doesn't mean Victoria can. *Hands off my baby sister!*

I always knew there were mean people in the world. But I never realized that a friend could be so mean, and then just keep going on with her life, all *la-la-la*, like she didn't even do the meanness that she just truly did.

I know I promised Mrs. Porridge that I wouldn't give up on Victoria, but right now I can't remember why that girl and I became friends in the first place. Victoria loves dressing up, being admired, and bossing people around. I love dogs, cheese and crackers, Hopper, my family (most of the time), playing my accordion, and kicking soccer balls with the bully twins (but that last one might upset Hopper if I admitted it out loud).

Victoria and I have nothing in common, so why can't I just ignore her? Hopper ignores almost everybody, but I can't seem to ignore anybody. Especially this girl.

Twenty-nine
Hopper

I look out the living room window and wait for the school bus to bring Quinny back to me. But when it stops at our corner, only Piper gets off.

"Hopper?" It's Mom talking behind me. "Quinny's dad called to say she went to play with Victoria this afternoon."

Oh. But we made a plan. She said she was coming here today.

I turn away from the window and stare at the floor.

"Sorry, honey, maybe you guys can hang out tomorrow."

"I don't care." I shrug. "No big deal."

"Do you want some pistachio ice cream? Or a Popsicle?"

I shake my head.

"Well, you should probably go back upstairs and get some rest."

I don't feel like arguing with Mom, so I obey. If Quinny didn't want to come over, I wish she would have told me so I didn't waste my whole day looking forward to it.

Soon I hear Dad's car pulling up the driveway and then him thumping up the stairs.

"Hey, buddy." Dad smiles at me from my doorway. He's got his work suit on, but his tie is loose. He looks eager. I don't have a good feeling about this.

"I came home early to take Ty and Trev over to the game—wanna come watch?"

I don't answer.

"Caleb's going to be there, too."

Hearing that makes me feel even worse.

"My throat is still healing," I finally say. "I'd better stay home and rest."

Dad steps into my room. "You felt good enough to go play with those chickens this morning," he points out.

"I wasn't playing, I was helping. Quinny's been doing it all by herself lately."

"Come on, Hopper—it'll be fun. Caleb's parents invited us all out for ice cream after."

That means I'd have to stay for the whole game. I don't know Caleb that well.

"Hopper?" Dad is waiting for me to say something.

But I'm still thinking about Caleb. He doesn't tease or hassle people, like Alex Delgado does. But if he keeps hanging out with Alex, he'll probably start to do that stuff, too, sooner or later. I really don't want to get sucked into all that. I also get the feeling sometimes that Caleb is nice to me because my brothers are soccer stars in our town. They're on a team that usually wins, and they've been in the newspaper before.

"Hopper, what do you say?" Dad is still looking at me, hopeful.

Why can't he leave me alone? He's always

saying what a fast runner I am and that soccer has lots of running. But it also has yelling, pushing, and crowds. I don't like that stuff. I don't like always having to win, especially while a crowd of grown-ups wants you to win so bad that they yell their guts out. I've been to my brothers' games. That's what it's like.

"No thank you," I repeat.

Dad throws his hands up. "Okay, fine."

"Jason, don't." Mom comes into my room now. "He's not fully healed yet."

"No one expects him to run around. Come on, Hopper—even Quinny loves going to soccer games. She pushed to come with us on Saturday, and she had a blast."

But Quinny told me they forced her to go to that game. I get chills down my back.

Mom smiles at me and pulls Dad away. "Just get some rest, sweetie," she says.

I hear them arguing in the hall.

"Be reasonable. He just had surgery," Mom whispers.

"It's not like I asked him to run laps!" Dad

doesn't whisper. "It's a beautiful day. Sorry for trying to spend time with my son—"

"You're pushing too hard, Jason. He's still recovering."

"Well, fine. Let him stay home and recover. Let him stay in that room his whole life and *stagnate*, if that's what he . . . but it'd be nice if he gave *something* a try at some point!"

Something? I guess juggling doesn't count and drawing doesn't count. Dad thinks my science books are weird, my anatomy models are weird, my aquarium is boring. Nothing counts unless it's something *he* likes, something that's about sports and crowds and noise.

And Mom doesn't say he's wrong. I listen for her voice. She feels bad, I can tell, but Dad talks right over her. It's almost like she agrees with him, deep down.

I get in bed and pull the covers over my head so I can't hear them argue.

Not as much, at least.

In the hospital, it felt like my parents loved me just for being me. Just for being alive. It felt like I belonged to my family for once, even to my brothers. My throat hurt and I felt sick from the surgery, but I didn't feel alone, and that was such a good, rare feeling.

That feeling's gone now. I don't think it'll ever come back.

Thirty
Quinny

I almost fall asleep on the way home from the playdate. Being with Victoria is exhausting.

But when we get home, I perk up and head over to Hopper's house.

"Quinny, no, it's almost dinnertime." Daddy blocks my way.

"But Hopper's probably wondering where I went!"

"I called his house to explain."

"Plus I need to tell him that Mrs. Flavio is letting us do the tonsils book together."

"You can tell him tomorrow. Calm down."

Daddy forces me home. I go upstairs and into

my old room (which is now Piper's room) and look out the window. Hopper's window is a little open and his shade is half up, but his light is off. Is he in there? Is he asleep?

There's only one way to find out. I pull out the Super Soaker water blaster from beneath my bed (where I hid it, because I'm not supposed to have water toys up here in the first place). Luckily, there's still a tiny bit of water left in it from summer. I aim that Super Soaker at Hopper's window, right into the open part.

Pump, pump, pump! Spray, spray, spray!

I wait. Then I wave, because there's Hopper at his window—looking a little damp, a little startled. This Super Soaker is *way* better at getting his attention than a call or a knock.

"Hopper, Hopper, Hopper! Guess what! Mrs. Flavio said we could—"

But he shuts his window in the middle of my sentence and pulls his shade down.

"Out." Piper comes into my/her room. "You're dress-passing."

I turn and glare at her. "It's pronounced

*tres*passing and this is still my room," I inform her. "I just did Mom and Dad a favor because *you know why*—"

"Get out!"

Piper kicks me in the butt, so I kick *her* in the butt. Then she howls, but I howl harder, but then she howls even harder. Then Daddy comes in and stops all the butt-kicking and howling, and I get another lecture about *setting a good example*.

In the middle of that lecture, Daddy notices the Super Soaker. And suddenly I'm in a whole new puddle of trouble.

I frown through dinner. I sulk through all the bedtime books. I trudge back upstairs to brush my teeth, and then I crawl under my covers.

Sometimes the best part of the day is when it's finally over.

Later, when I'm supposed to be asleep, I still can't sleep. I think about Victoria.

All those lies I told her about our book being published by a fake publisher.

All that pretending that I can go to her party when I already have plans with Hopper.

206

All the yuck she makes me feel in the bottom of my stomach almost every day.

Why am I still curious about her even when she's so awful? Why does something about her just poke at my heart? Why did I make Mrs. Porridge that promise?

I think about Victoria's huge house and her dead mother and her dead mother's dead cat. I think about how I would never stop crying if I had a dead mother and a dead cat and an empty house with a daddy who works all the time and only a Masha for company (even though she seems nice). But Victoria is no crybaby. She gets stuff done. I wish I were as gutsy and sure about everything as she is.

The only thing that distracts me from Victoria is Cleo's sleepy snuffles.

I get up and go over to her crib. Watching her breathe makes my own breathing slow down. I lean over and sniff that baby sister—a little sweet, a little sour, and oh so warm. I climb into her crib again. I bend my knees to fit around her all cozy, and it's like sleeping with a real live supersoft stuffed animal who doesn't have any problems at all. Nothing bad has ever happened to Cleo. I love that about her. I wish we could switch places maybe. Her mini hand is fat and silky, and it fits perfectly inside my giant regular hand. Her mini fluttery heart beats against my tummy.

They don't tell you when you're little, but being a baby is simple.

It's growing up that's the hard part.

Thirty-one

Hopper

It's three in the morning, and my eyes won't stay shut.

I get up and look up the word *stagnate* in my dictionary.

STAGNATE: to become inactive
or still; to stop developing,
progressing, moving

So that's what Dad thinks I'm doing in here. Not juggling, drawing, reading, thinking.

I look over at my chess set, my fish tank, my model of a human eye. I pick up my juggling sacks and toss them up into a three-ball cascade. Then I throw them at my door.

Dad's wrong. I'm not who he thinks I am.

I look out my window. Quinny feels so far away. She doesn't sleep in the room across from my room anymore. She didn't come over yesterday, like she said she would. She wasn't forced to go to my brothers' soccer game, like she said she was. She went on purpose. She had a blast and lied about it.

Dad isn't the only one who's wrong. Quinny isn't who I thought she was, either.

Maybe no one really is.

Thirty-two

Quinny

Disco's *creeecreeecreee*-ing wakes up the whole neighborhood again on Thursday. Maybe even the whole town. That chicken obviously didn't listen to a word I said.

The first thing I need to do this morning is find Hopper and explain why I didn't show up yesterday. But Mom won't let me knock on his door before breakfast. I don't see him at the chicken porch, either. Then Daddy says we can't stop by Hopper's house on the way to the bus because we're running late (again).

Phooey.

But the good news is, it's early dismissal in school today! Which I totally forgot about, and which means Hopper and I will have extra time this afternoon to catch up on all the tonsils book stuff we wanted to do yesterday.

More good news: Victoria kind of leaves me alone today. She still watches me, but she doesn't pounce on me at recess, so I spend it kicking a soccer ball with Caleb and Alex and some other kids. And hey, I can actually sort of keep up with those boys.

They run faster than me, but my feet are trickier than theirs.

Their bodies are pushy, but mine is twistier.

And nobody kicks that ball harder than me.

Tricky feet + a twisty body + one good hard kick = GOAL!

I imagine the crowd cheering and clapping.

"Wow, so are you going to join the soccer team or what?" Caleb asks.

"Big Mouth on my team? No way." Alex chortles.

Alex started calling me *Big Mouth* because he heard the bully twins do it. Not cool.

"Maybe I'll join a different team so I can destroy you guys every time," I say.

"Ooh, burn." He rolls his eyes and smirks.

I can handle these boys. Kicking a ball around with them actually makes me happier than playing with Victoria. This is the most fun I've had at recess since Hopper was in school.

But there's also grumpy news today.

After recess, Victoria comes up to me and says "I hope you enjoyed running around with those grubby boys, because tomorrow you're playing with us again."

Huh?

"It's only fair to take turns," she adds. "One day you'll play with boys, the next you'll play with us. I'll help you keep track of the schedule."

I don't want her help. I want to do what I want to do. That's what recess is for.

And right now I want to yell at Victoria to LEAVE ME ALONE. But we're about to start math and Mrs. Flavio is up by the whiteboard, and I don't want to get into any more trouble with that sub, especially since she gave me back my recess in the first place.

When I get to Hopper's house after school, the bad news keeps going. I tell him all the exciting stuff he missed yesterday: how Mrs. Flavio gave me back my recess, and how she's letting us do the tonsils book together after all. And I say sorry that I couldn't come over the day before. But nothing I say makes a dent in Hopper's frown.

"Did you have fun at Victoria's house?" He scowls at me.

"Sorry, I told you, Daddy forced me to go."

"Right."

"Hopper, it's true."

"Just like my brothers *forced* you to go to that soccer game on Saturday?"

Hmmm . . . I don't know what to say now.

214

Hopper looks at my face close-up. "Tell the truth, Quinny. You wanted to go to the soccer game. And you wanted to go to Victoria's house. You don't have to lie about it."

Wow. Hopper really thinks I'm a liar. He doesn't even know the biggest lie I've been telling lately. Or how scared I am to un-tell that lie.

I feel like that boy's words just slapped me in the face.

But then why is he the one who looks ready to cry?

Thirty-three

Hopper

There's no reason to cry. I'm not upset at Quinny. It's not her fault my father wants to change my whole personality.

"Dad said you pushed to go to the soccer game. He said you love soccer."

"I didn't push," says Quinny. "The twins invited me."

"Is it true? Do you love soccer?"

She doesn't say anything.

"It's okay if you say yes."

"I'm curious about soccer, that's all."

"Why?"

"Why am I curious about soccer?"

"Yeah, why?" I'm staring at her so much now. It's rude, but I don't care.

"I don't know," she says. "Maybe it's kind of the same reason I love New York City, and my accordion, and running down to breakfast in the morning. It just feels exciting."

Quinny smiles. Even her nose is smiling. It crinkles up like her accordion.

"And being on a team sounds fun. When you're happy about winning, you have a whole bunch of kids to be happy with. And if you lose, you can all feel droopy together."

Excitement. Togetherness. I get it. I wish I felt it the way she does.

"I think my dad would rather have you for a kid than me," I whisper.

Quinny looks shocked now. I tell her about yesterday, how my dad acted. And that's when I start to cry for real. She hugs me. I'm embarrassed, but it's okay. It's just Quinny.

"Geez, Hopper, I can't believe you had that whole big fight about soccer."

"He wants me to be like him. All he cares about is winning."

"Winning is fun." Quinny shrugs. "But lots of other things are fun, too."

"It's not fair. If you're a boy, you have to do sports. If you're a girl, it's like a choice."

Quinny says that wasn't true back in New York City.

"I knew lots of boys who didn't do sports. . . . They did things like music or drama or robotics. I knew a boy at my old school who did ballet, and another one who made a whole village out of Legos for some contest that he won and he even beat a lot of older kids."

"Well, around here, if you don't do sports, it's not so great for you."

"Sorry, Hopper, that stinks. I don't care what you do, as long as it makes you happy."

Just hearing Quinny say that makes me feel better. Talking about how it stinks makes it stink a little bit less.

All of a sudden, Quinny's eyes pop huge. "Wait. . . . Hopper, isn't juggling a sport?"

"No."

"Well, it should be! It's hard to do, it makes you tired, and people love to watch."

"Ha. No, juggling is more like a circus act."

"Oh, plus also, Hopper, you're a really good runner, and that's a sport."

"Running isn't a sport."

"It totally is—"

"No, it's something you do in other sports, like baseball or basketball—"

"No, running is a sport all by itself! Hello? Haven't you heard of track and field? And marathons, where you run, like, a zillion miles in a row? And swimming—now, that for sure is a sport. I remember over the summer Grandpa Gooley said you're a strong swimmer."

I love to swim, but I don't care about swimming faster than other people. There's something wrong with me that I don't care about that. Normal people care about winning. Normal people are more like Dad, and Quinny, and my brothers, and Victoria.

Victoria cares about winning and being number one at life.

Alex Delgado cares about it bad. I'm pretty sure Caleb does, too.

"Let's work on finishing our book," says Quinny. "I bet that will take your mind off all this grumpy stuff."

So we do. And she's right—it does.

Thirty-four

Quinny

I hop onto the school bus in a great mood, and not just because today is Friday.

Today Daddy is picking me up after school, and we're going straight to Dr. Merkle's office so Hopper and I can show him our amazing, brand-new tonsils book!

Even Victoria can't spoil my good mood. She tries pretty hard, though. At recess, she makes me come to another meeting to plan her costume party. I try to work up the courage to tell her I can't go to her party, but recess ends before I do. I want to start saying only things that are truly true from now on, but it's harder than it looks.

Mrs. Porridge has agreed to watch my little sisters after school so Daddy can drive me to Dr. Merkle's office. It's super rare for me to get Daddy all to myself, so I try to make the most of it.

"Hey, let's go to the animal shelter afterward," I say in the car.

"Quinny, please."

"Just kidding. I know that's never, ever gonna happen."

Daddy groans.

"It's okay. Pretty soon I'll be all grown up and I can adopt a dog of my own."

At Dr. Merkle's office, Hopper introduces me to everyone as his "co-author" and we show them our book. All thirty-seven pages of it, with a snazzy cover and everything.

"What a great idea," says Dr. Merkle. "Laughter is the best medicine, indeed."

Trudy, who works behind the front desk, says, "You kids are so creative. And, Hopper, we had no idea you were such an amazing artist."

"He doesn't tell anyone," I inform them. "He's a genius at lots of secret things."

"She's the one who made the book so good," Hopper says. "Dr. Merkle, do you really think you can use it for other kids?"

Dr. Merkle smiles. "I think it would make a fine addition to our waiting-room reading rack. How thoughtful to help others going through a tonsillectomy. I'm proud of you guys."

"Hold up the book and smile!" Trudy yells.

She wants to take a picture of me and Hopper and Dr. Merkle. It's like we're the most famous people inside this whole doctor's office.

"Cheeeeeeeeese!" I call out.

But I don't think Hopper is really smiling, so I tickle him as a gentle reminder.

On our way out, Dr. Merkle says, "Would you mind if we make some copies of this?"

"Not at all," I say. "We were hoping you would do that."

"The ads are my favorite part," says Dr. Merkle, flipping through the book. "You're a couple of comedians, aren't you?"

"She's the funny one." Hopper kicks at my foot.

"No, you're really funny. You just don't let people know."

"You came up with all the best stuff in there," Hopper insists.

Well, okay, if he says so!

When we're done meeting with Dr. Merkle, Hopper's mom says, "Kids, I think this calls for a celebration. How about a pizza party at our house?"

Hopper and I look at each other. He smiles, too late for the camera, and we holler a *YES!* and run down the hall to the elevators. We worked hard and did something good together, and it feels awesome.

On the ride home, I think about what a great friend that boy is. He gave me credit for the funny things in the book. He told everyone how hard I worked. He's loyal and careful with people's feelings. Hopper would never skip my birthday to go to someone else's big, fancy party. He would never do that. So why would I even think about doing that to him?

"Daddy, can we make just one quick stop on the way home?" I ask.

A few minutes later, Daddy pulls up to Victoria's wedding cake house.

"I'll be right back." I get out of the car.

"Quinny? Wait, you can't just . . . Wait for me!"

But I'm already halfway to Victoria's front door. I told Daddy I forgot a sweater here on our playdate. Which is another lie I told. The last one ever, I hope.

Now it's time to tell the truth, the whole truth, and nothing but the truth.

Victoria is surprised to see me at her front door. She smiles and touches her hair.

I'm surprised she gets to answer her front door. I expected her Masha to open it.

"Victoria, it's me, good evening. I have something important to tell you, and please don't interrupt or I'll lose my courage. I can't go to your party because I already have plans with Hopper and I should have told you that before, but I was afraid you'd get mad, plus your party sounded really great, and I wish I could be in two places at once, but I can't, so that's why I can't go to your party or help plan a menu for it. Sorry. Plus, also, my book isn't really being published by ENT Books Corporation, I lied about that, too."

Victoria looks . . . amused? Which is a surprise. Like half amused, half hurt.

"I knew it," she says. "I knew you'd pick him."

She tries to shut the door in my face, but I stop it from shutting and follow her inside her house. "Victoria, what are you talking about?"

"Hopper," Victoria huffs. "He's so boring. He doesn't have any friends and he isn't even having a real birthday party, so you invited him to New York City, which is a waste of time—you'd have so much more fun going to New York with me."

"Wait, so you knew about my plans with Hopper? And you still made your party at the same time, like, on purpose?"

Victoria shrugs.

"But that's so . . ." Rude and horrible. Plus icky and mean. "It's his birthday—we're going to a big science event he's really excited about."

"You know, I like science, too. I'm just as smart as Hopper—my grades are excellent!"

"Who cares about your perfect grades? You're a bad friend!"

Victoria takes a step back. My breath feels fast and hot, like my mouth is on fire.

"I'm sick of it!" I yell. "The way you force everybody to do life your way. You're not in charge of the world! You don't get to boss my recess around and act all horrible—"

"I'm not horrible."

"If you're not horrible, then why do you act all horrible?"

Victoria looks at me, confused. "I don't."

"You do! You're a rude, braggy, bossy meanie who makes everybody miserable, and school would be a nicer place without you!"

I stand there, shaking. Did all those awful words really just burst out of me?

Victoria takes another step back. She whimpers and turns and runs up the stairs.

Her Masha is by the stairs with a shocked look on her face.

"Quinny, what just happened?" Daddy is behind me now. "Where's your sweater?"

What happened was, I don't even know. But it

didn't make things better. It felt like scratching a mosquito bite: really great for a few seconds but a lot more painful after.

I was meaner than Victoria. I out-meaned Victoria Porridge. I made her *whimper.*

"I just want to go home. Can we please go?"

At home, I don't want pizza or people or anything, because my stomach hurts. I just want to lie down by myself. There is a deep ocean of awfulness inside me that I didn't even know was there. And I think I'm drowning in it.

Eventually, I get up to use the bathroom, and I overhear Mom on the phone.

"I can't believe a third grader would be that hurtful," she says. "How disappointing. I've always thought of her as a kind girl. We need to have a talk, that's for sure."

I don't know if Mom is talking about me or Victoria. It's so weird to think she might be talking about me. I never thought of myself as a mean person. I try to be kind to other people. But I wasn't kind to Victoria.

Is it okay to be mean to someone who was mean to you first?

I'm not sure, but I think my stomachache knows the answer.

Thirty-five

Hopper

Mom and I make the best pizza.

We squish and stretch fresh dough. We chop and prep stuff for a toppings bar. Tonight we put out all of Quinny's favorites: pickles, bacon, Nutella.

Mom asks me to set the table and fill water glasses and call my brothers. When my brothers don't come, she yells for them to turn off the video game and wash hands now.

Then we all wait for Quinny.

"Why do we have to wait for Big Mouth?" Trevor grumbles.

"Trevor, stop," says Mom. "Her name is Quinny."

"She's the co-author of my book," I say. "That's why we're having a pizza party."

Finally, Mom calls Quinny's house. When she

gets off the phone, she looks confused. "Quinny's not feeling well, and she's decided to skip the pizza."

"But she was feeling fine at Dr. Merkle's office."

"I'm sorry, sweetheart. Now, apparently, she's not."

So I eat with my brothers. They don't care one bit about our tonsils book. They mess up the toppings bar. It's definitely not as fun as having a pizza party with my co-author.

Afterward, I go back upstairs by myself. I adjust the pH level in my fish tank. I juggle.

I take apart my anatomy model of a human heart and put it back together. I know it so well that I can almost do it with my eyes closed.

I sit there, with my eyes closed, wondering what's wrong with Quinny.

Then there's a knock at my door.

But it doesn't sound like Quinny. This knock is gentler.

"Who is it?"

"It's me," says a tiny voice.

I open the door and see Piper staring up at me.

"What are you doing here? Where's Quinny?"

Piper walks into my room. She picks up the chess set by my desk.

"Is Quinny okay? She was supposed to come over."

Piper opens the chess set. She looks at me and waits.

"It's not as easy as checkers," I warn her.

"I know. I could tell." She glances over at my window. "What are the rules?"

I go and sit across from Piper. We line up the chess pieces on the board.

"These ones, they're called bishops," I say. "And these are the king and queen."

Saturday morning, I go over to Quinny's house.

"Sorry, Hopper, she's still not feeling well," her mom says.

"Where?"

"Excuse me?"

"Where in her body isn't she feeling well? There's all kinds of medicine to help."

Quinny's mom ignores my question. "We'll call as soon as she's on the mend. I promise."

On my way home, I hear someone whistle from

the street. It's Grandpa Gooley in his truck. "Heading over to the chickens," he says. "Care to lend a hand?"

I go over to Mrs. Porridge's yard and lend him both of my hands. The *chalet des poulets* is almost done. I help put the finishing touches on it.

"Truly a thing of beauty," says Grandpa Gooley, standing back to admire it.

Then we go up onto the porch to let the chickens know their new home is ready.

It feels good to be up here. If I squint, I can almost see Quinny dancing in the corner.

But then Disco lunges at Walter and tries to peck his eyes out.

Walter hisses at Disco and tries to scratch his face off.

Mrs. Porridge comes out, picks up Walter, and carries him into the house. She gives me and Grandpa Gooley a look, like we're bonkers to build a fancy coop for these maniacs.

"Well, even if the critters are out of sorts today, we should still celebrate." Grandpa Gooley looks at me as we walk outside. "Hopper, what do you say to a donut? I bet the farmers' market probably has a few left."

I shrug. "I do nut know what to say to a donut."

"Har-har. Where'd you get your sense of humor, a garage sale?"

Then Mom's voice interrupts us. "Hopper?" She's walking up to us. "Come with me. Daddy and I need to talk to you about something."

She looks serious. So does Dad when we get back home.

Is this about Quinny? Is something wrong with Quinny?

"Hopper, did you go on Mom's computer this week without asking?" Dad asks.

I don't answer his question. He slips a paper in front of me. It's the e-mail I sent to Principal Ramsey earlier this week while Mom was in the basement doing laundry.

An e-mail I sent from her computer, without permission.

An e-mail I'm not supposed to know how to send, but I figured it out.

To: sramsey@wves.edu
From: carolinegrey@zmail.com
Wednesday, October 6; 9:37 am

Principal Ramsey,

This is Hopper Grey. I have two topics I'm writing about today.

Please give Quinny Bumble back her recess is my first topic. She is very upset. Recess detention is against the rules. My friend Owen's mom figured that out a couple of years ago when his older brother kept losing recess. She looked it up. Please tell Mrs. Flavio this. Also, Quinny has a really fast engine. She needs to wiggle so she can calm down and learn. This is a proven fact.

I know Quinny doesn't always behave. One idea is to make Quinny run laps at recess instead of taking away her recess.

The second topic I am writing about is the how-to writing assignment. Mrs. Flavio said we cannot do my tonsillectomy book together. Quinny and I want to do this topic together because teamwork is important. Quinny has a lot of great ideas. Quinny has worked very hard to help me with this, and it is not fair to take that away from her. Thank you for reading my e-mail.

Your student, Hopper Grey

"Look familiar?" asks Dad.

"You know you're not allowed on the computer without a grown-up," says Mom.

I do know that.

"You broke into my personal e-mail account. Who taught you to do that?"

I didn't have to do much breaking. Because her password is *PASSWORD*.

"Hopper, what do you have to say for yourself?"

"Sorry." I hang my head and wait to hear my punishment. Maybe they'll ban me from the computer forever. Maybe they'll take away my playdates with Quinny.

Then Mom slips another paper in front of me. "This came yesterday," she says.

To: carolinegrey@zmail.com
From: sramsey@wves.edu
Friday, October 8; 4:32 pm

Hopper,
Thank you for your note. I appreciate you taking the time to share your point of view. Quinny is lucky to have you as a friend. Please know that at Whisper Valley Elementary

237

School, we strive to be fair and do what is right. I have reviewed our policy prohibiting recess detention with all school staff. Also, after talking with Mrs. Flavio, we have decided to allow you and Quinny to work together on the language arts assignment.

I wish you a speedy recovery from your tonsillectomy and look forward to seeing you back in the halls soon.

Sincerely,

Principal Ramsey

I can't believe Principal Ramsey read my e-mail and wrote me back.

I look at Mom and Dad. They're smiling now. "So I'm not in trouble?"

"For using my computer without permission, yes, you are," says Mom.

"But you stuck up for a friend. You tried to help," says Dad. "You showed initiative, and that's a big deal, Hopper. That's a really big deal to me."

I remind myself to look up *initiative* later. But I can tell it means something good.

"And about the other night," Dad continues. "I'm sorry, I shouldn't have pushed you to go to the game. I just want you to be happy and have fun, and . . ."

And be more like you. I finish the sentence in my mind.

Dad hugs me. I can tell he feels sorry. And Mom looks happy to see us hugging. I wonder if anything will really change, though, after this hug. I hope so.

"Ahh-hem." Grandpa Gooley comes into the room. "If you folks are done with my grandson, I believe there's a donut with his name on it at the farmers' market."

There isn't really, but there is a donut with maple syrup and bacon on it. I get two of those—one for me, and one to save for Quinny, who is bacon's biggest fan.

I'm sitting on a bench with Grandpa Gooley and eating my donut when he pulls out a card from his wallet. "You're looking at the newest member of the YMCA in Nutley," he says.

Nutley is bigger than Whisper Valley. We don't go there much since it is two towns away and doesn't have a soccer dome. But I've heard their YMCA has a giant pool.

"Look what else I got." He hands me another card, with bright stripes on it. "It was a special offer, too good to pass up. A free year of membership for anyone in third or fourth grade."

I look at the card. It says YMCA YOUTH MEMBER. And also my name.

"Doc says I need more exercise. I sure could use some company."

"Are you kidding? Grandpa Gooley, you just built a whole chicken coop."

"The other interesting thing is, the Y has a junior swim team. For kids ten and up."

I'm only turning nine this month. *Phew.*

"I know you're not ten yet, but free swim's open to everybody," he says. "Think about it: we could swim year-round, Hopper. What do you say?"

I shrug at this. It does sound pretty great, actually. "But I don't want to do any races."

"You know what's good about swimming? You can compete against yourself. Against your own best time, without worrying about other people or races."

"How would I know how fast I was going?"

"Well, I suppose I could time you."

"I'm only fast when no one's looking."

"I bet you could still be fast when people are looking, Hopper. I bet you really could."

As Quinny would say, there's only one way to find out.

Thirty-six

Quinny

I can't even remember how long I've been lying here.

Mom comes in and tries to talk to me again. She sort of knows what happened with Victoria, but wants me to tell her in my own words. For once in my life, I don't have words.

Later, she brings me a bowl of cereal, which turns to mush on my bedside table.

She brings me an apple that I'm too sad to bite into.

She tries to make me go watch Saturday morning cartoons with Piper.

When I say no to that, she takes my temperature.

Then she brings me Cleo, who I cuddle because it's impossible not to cuddle Cleo.

Why did I yell at Victoria like that? I feel bad for yelling, but I'm still mad at her, too.

I didn't know a person could feel so guilty and so angry at the same time.

It feels a lot like a stomach bug.

I give that baby sister back to Mom and go back to sleep.

Later Saturday afternoon, Daddy comes in and sits on my bed.

"So how about that trip to the animal shelter?" he says.

A tiny part of me perks up. But most of me just slumps there still.

I turn over and look at the wall. That's my answer.

"Wow," says Daddy.

Later, Mom comes in and makes me slurp some soup. She says she knows friendship can be hard and sometimes we all make mistakes, but talking things through will help.

243

But I'm too ashamed to talk about how I yelled at Victoria. And at how *true* the things I yelled still feel. I'm a bad person for feeling such bad feelings.

I didn't think Victoria and I had anything in common, but we do. We're both rotten.

It gets dark out. Which matches how I feel, which actually makes me feel a bit better.

"I just want to sleep," I tell Mom. "Thank you for the soup."

"Quinny? Quinny, wake up."

Mom's back. It's light out again. I scrunch my eyes and moan when she raises my blinds. "Quinny, time to wake up—it's Sunday. Come on, we let you sleep all morning."

I pull the covers over my head.

"Quinny, listen. Disco is leaving this afternoon—"

I whip those covers off. "What? Why?"

"You know why."

"But, Mom, it's not her fault she's a rooster."

"No, it's not. But *he's* getting too loud and aggressive to live here anymore. Mrs. Porridge said he tried to attack Walter again yesterday—"

"That happens all the time. Friendship can be hard—you said it yourself."

"Walter and Disco are most certainly not friends," says Mom.

"How do you know? Maybe they just need some help talking things through—"

"Ha."

"I'm serious!"

"Quinny, if you want to say good-bye, I suggest you get up and go brush your teeth."

"I'm not saying good-bye." I roll over and kick the wall.

"Suit yourself. But if you let Disco leave without saying good-bye, you might regret it."

Mom leaves. I kick the wall again. Then I get up and go brush my teeth.

I pass the empty *chalet des poulets* and the empty porch coop. Everybody is by Grandpa Gooley's truck, with a chicken crate that is full of Disco.

"Disco!" I run toward that trapped rooster. "Let her out!"

Mrs. Porridge catches me before I get to Disco.

She holds me in a hug. Then, slowly, she walks me over to Disco's crate.

"Good-bye, Disco," I sniffle.

"Screeee-cawreeeeee."

When Disco and Cha-Cha first got here, I pictured a whole flock of fluffy, friendly chickens, and lots of conversation, and lots of eggs. I thought there'd be fat, happy birds everywhere, acting silly and making us laugh. Now there's just an empty coop, and one confused chicken in love with a crabby cat, and one noisy rooster who's getting kicked out.

"So much for raising chickens," I grump. "Now we have nothing."

"Let's look at what we do have, Quinny," says Mrs. Porridge. "Look how much Cha-Cha loves Walter. I never thought anyone besides me would love Walter, but he's found someone who does. A friend. And that's a beautiful thing, even if they aren't both chickens."

"What's going to happen to Disco?" I ask.

"He's moving to a farm where he'll get to be who he truly is—he can't do that here."

"But Grandpa Gooley built that giant chicken coop."

"And he did a good job."

"Just a good job?" says Grandpa Gooley.

"Don't push your luck, mister," Mrs. Porridge snaps.

"Can we get more chickens?" I ask.

"Over my dead body," she declares.

"I think that's a maybe," says Grandpa Gooley.

I stare over at the empty *chalet des poulets*. Cha-Cha and Walter don't even seem interested in it. "This isn't how I pictured it would happen."

"Sometimes you have to let go of what you thought would happen," says Mrs. Porridge, "and live the life that's actually happening . . . the life you're in."

"But isn't that the opposite of 'dream big'?"

Mrs. Porridge looks confused.

"At school, there is a big sign in the hallway telling us to dream big. But if we just accept whatever happens, that means we're not dreaming big."

"Ah, you have to do both, Quinny. The trick to being a person is you have to do both."

There's something else I'm worried about, too. I want to believe that Disco is going to a farm where he will boss a whole flock of hens around and be happy. But when grown-ups say an animal *went to live on a farm*, sometimes they really mean something worse.

"You're probably just going to drive Disco around the block," I say to Grandpa Gooley. "And then Mrs. Porridge is going to boil him up for dinner, right?"

Mrs. Porridge looks shocked. "Quinny, first of all, I'm a vegetarian. Second, we searched high and low for a good home for Disco. Are you calling us liars?"

I stare up at Mrs. Porridge's offended face. "No, ma'am."

"If I was going to boil Disco up for dinner, believe me, I'd let you know," she huffs. "Do I look like someone who would lie to protect you from the harsh realities of life? Is that the kind of deceptive, mushy-hearted person you think I am?"

"No, I guess not . . . except, maybe."

"Bite your tongue, Quinny," she snaps. "Bite it hard."

But I think Mrs. Porridge tries to hide her real personality as much as Hopper does. Luckily, I have special X-ray eyeballs that can see right through to her secret mushy heart.

"Better hit the road," says Grandpa Gooley.

"Can I have a moment with Disco?" I ask him.

"Of course."

I sit with that rooster by the pickup truck. "Disco, it's okay. Go and be your true self. But don't forget about us here, okay? We still love you, and we're never going to forget you."

"Never, ever," says Piper, coming up to us now. She's carrying my accordion.

"One last song?" she asks, handing me that accordion.

"One last song," I agree, slipping it onto my arms. "Any requests?"

"Brrrrrrifff," says Cha-Cha, nearby. *"Buuu bip."*

"Screeeeeeee," replies Disco.

I play "Let It Be," my favorite sad song in the world. It fills me up with such sad joy.

I don't sing the words, but Piper and Mrs. Porridge do. Afterward, Disco lets us hug him and stroke his feathers. Piper cries. Which is actually a good thing, because then I have to be the mature big sister and take care of Piper's feelings, so I forget to cry myself.

Grandpa Gooley finally drives Disco away.

We wave good-bye one last time. Then we have a very, very, extra-very sad walk home.

I run upstairs to go cry in my bed.

But before I get there, I see a sign in the hall that directs me back to my *old* room.

And when I arrive at my old room, my old bed looks made up the way it used to be, with my comforter and pillow and everything—like it's my very own bed again!

Plus there's a cage by the window. And something is shuffling and scampering inside. It's furry, with brown and white spots, and a tiny pink nose. Bigger than a hamster, smaller than a kitten. And cuter than anything I've ever seen in my whole entire life.

"Mommy, come look—there's a . . . what is it? Ooh, is that a guinea pig? Mom, look! There's a guinea pig in the house! Where on earth did that precious thing come from?"

"Indoor voice, Quinny. It's from the animal shelter. We're just fostering him."

"So you mean he's not really mine? Or he is?"

"We have to see how Piper reacts, with her allergies. But the doctor seemed to think that one guinea pig wouldn't be a big issue."

I stick my fingers into the cage. The piggy sniffs them hello. He looks a little shy, but his eyes are full of love. Like he needs me to love him back right this very minute.

"Piper, I have a big favor to ask. Please don't be allergic to this sweet piggy, please?"

"Okay," she says. "But only if it's half mine." She sticks her fingers into the cage, too.

"Can we take him out of the cage?" I ask Mom.

"I guess so, but be careful."

I take the piggy out of the cage, and he's cooing and snuffling on my lap and doesn't even try to run away. I hold him close and Piper pets him, too.

"Let's see how it goes," says Mom. "We'll know more in a few days."

But I already know. In my heart I know this

piggy is here to stay. I had no idea I even wanted a guinea pig, but now I realize this is exactly the pet I've always wanted.

"Oh, Mom, I know that doctor is right! Look, Piper's not even sneezing. Thank you so much from the bottom of my—"

"Don't thank me, Quinny. This was all Victoria's idea."

"Victoria?"

"She saw the guinea pig at the shelter and thought it'd be a good solution for us."

"She did? Is she here? Victoria?"

"No, but she sent you this." Mom hands me a note.

A lump bumps up in my throat. I hand Piper the guinea pig so I can read that note. It's in swoopy cursive on fancy stationery that matches Victoria's business cards.

Quinny,

I know I did a bad thing with the party. I'm sorry. I will try harder to be a nice friend. Can you please try harder, too? You really hurt my feelings. I wish you were as nice to me as you

are to Hopper, because I have a lot to offer. I am
fun, creative, and generous. Also, I can make
any snack you want if you come over to my
house again, even if it has dairy. We just have
to ask Masha in advance.

    Sincerely,

    Victoria Rose Porridge

The note makes me want to write her a note
back. Or talk to her, because I'm sorry, too, and I
have a lot to say, and it would take a lot of paper
to explain it all.

But I'm not sure if I can ever trust Victoria
again. Or if she can trust me. I promised Mrs.
Porridge I wouldn't give up on our friendship, but
I don't know if I can fix all this hurt.

I show Victoria's note to my new piggy and ask
for his advice. But he just tries to nibble on it. I
show him all around my room, and then the whole
world out my window.

And there's Hopper at his window, looking
back at us. He's got slicked-back, greasy hair, for
some reason, like an old-fashioned 1950s Hopper.

I open my window. "Hopper, there you are!

Meet my brand-new guinea pig! He's so new he doesn't even have a name yet! Also, why is your hair slicked back like that?"

Hopper waves. "Take a wild guess." He points over to the window next to his, which is a bathroom window. And inside it is Trevor, scowling with a flowery shower cap on his head. Ty is behind him, sitting and getting his hair slimed with conditioner by his mom.

"Oh, Hopper, I'm sorry your family got fleas, too! By the way, Disco's gone," I call out. "You missed the whole thing."

"I said good-bye before, by myself. I'm not supposed to be around people's heads."

Oh sure, I know those rules pretty well by now.

The piggy squeaks and purrs in my hands. I hold him up, closer to the window.

"That's Hopper." I point. "He's a little shy, too, so I think you guys will get along great." I gesture over to those crabby boys in the bathroom window, both wearing puffy, flowery shower caps now. "And those are the bully twins, but you can't call them that, because it's rude. Their real names are Ty and Trevor. And tomorrow I'll introduce you to Walter and Cha-Cha. But they might try to eat you, especially Walter, so be careful at first, okay?"

The piggy whirrs and nestles against my chest, and twitches his tiny little pink nose, and my heart is on fire with joy, joy, joy.

"But right now, our first job is to figure out what your name is."

Thirty-seven
Hopper

I soak up Quinny's smile as she waves out her window.

Her new guinea pig is cute, but it looks kind of terrified.

I'm not sure what happened Friday night, but I'm glad to see her feeling better.

And I'm glad Mom's letting us reschedule our pizza party.

In the meantime, I think I'll go play some video games with my brothers, since all three of us caught lice. Which is not the same thing as fleas, no matter what Quinny says.

THE END

Epilogue

Quinny

But wait! There's more!

So Hopper's family finally got rid of those fleas, and life went back to normal, and now, a few weeks later, Hopper and I are finally going to the Brain Expo.

But not just by ourselves.

Hopper

It wasn't my idea to invite Victoria and Caleb to the Brain Expo. It was you-know-who's. To tell you the truth, I thought they'd say it sounded boring or stupid. But they said yes. Victoria even switched some party she was planning to a different time so she could come. The four of us are going into New York City today.

Quinny

Make that the *eight* of us. Because Piper threw a fit and wanted to come, too. And Mrs. Porridge is coming to keep an eye on Victoria—even though I told her that things have been much better lately with us at school.

Since it's a couple of days before Halloween, we can't just go in our regular clothes.

Hopper

There are some other people in costumes at the Brain Expo, but we're definitely the strangest-looking bunch here. We all dressed up because afterward we're going to a Halloween party at Quinny's old apartment building in the city.

But first we walk around the Brain Expo.

It's crowded and thrilling. But I'm surprised that the longest line here isn't to see the real human brain. It's to get into an exhibit called *It's All in Your Head*, where you get to walk through a giant pretend brain and see what it's like from the inside.

"That sounds really weird," says Victoria.

"It sounds kind of cool," says Caleb.

"Happy birthday, Professor Grey." Quinny smiles and nudges me.

"Happy Halloween, Dr. Bumble." I nudge her back.

Quinny's smile goes gruesome. "Excuse me, my name is Dr. Dead."

"Welcome to your head, Dr. Dead," says the man by *It's All in Your Head*.

Then I grab Quinny's hand and Piper's tiny one, too, and I lead the way inside.

THE **REAL** END